DAPHNE LEONIE WRIGHT

On Love

and Death

and Belonging

a novel

Daphne Leonie Wright
On Love and Death and Belonging

Softcover ISBN 978-1-7387424-0-0
Electronic ISBN (Kindle) 978-1-7387424-1-7
Audiobook 978-1-7387424-2-4

Book Cover Design | Yasmine Franchi
Book Interior Design | Petya Tsankova
Editor | Tara McGuire
Publishing Support | TSPA The Self Publishing Agency, Inc.

To John,
while it may be true that life doesn't get any easier,
with you it always gets better.

Contents

Winter/Spring 2019

Fiona

Head up, eyes forward, a self-imposed imaginary protective perimeter keeping her away from the zombie-like pedestrians meandering on the sidewalk, Fiona was on a mission. She quickened her pace. To anyone watching, it was a brisk walk. To Fiona, it was a run. Ahead of her, the #20 bus pulled away from the curb like an ocean liner leaving port. As it merged into the traffic of Commercial Drive, the usual accompanying squeals of braking and honking horns from drivers trying to outrun the bus were missing. Instead, the #20 joined the traffic heading south, leaving Fiona behind to wait.

Her mission aborted until the next bus, Fiona stopped running and, bending over, put her hands to her knees. Haaaa, deep breath out. Ahhum, deep breath in. Haaaa, deep breath out. Ahhum, deep breath in. *God, I sound like whale music. Those extra twenty pounds have got to go.* But like an old friend, Fiona knew those pounds weren't going anywhere. Her various diets had failed: low carb-high fat, high carb-low fat, watermelon and cabbage soup, nothing until lunch and then only fruit. More times than not, as the cakes and pies came out of their hiding place, any weight lost returned two-fold.

"I can't afford to gain any more weight going on a diet, Dr Chan." This said after being told she had a fifty-percent opportunity of a heart attack or stroke if things didn't change.

"Fiona, you're a nurse. You know better." Dr Chan admonished, adding a look back at the scale for emphasis. And that's what Fiona was hoping for at her doctor's appointment today. A chance to do better.

Fiona got to the bus stop. "Gotta smoke?" An older, scruffily-dressed man sitting on the bus bench asked, staring out onto the street as if searching for something lost. From his lip a lit cigarette dangled as the ash defied gravity.

"Sorry. No." Coughing, Fiona stepped back from the cloud of smoke drifting up to her face. "Besides, they'll kill you."

"I can only hope," the old man answered. A sentinel on watch, he continued to look out onto the street before him.

Fiona looked back the way she had come, hoping transit added a second bus. Instead, sauntering toward her, a man-boy taking sips from a Starbucks cup outstretched his left hand toward her in a gesture of want. Fiona's eyes moved downward to his sneakers, her way of discerning someone's personal economics. His shoes looked as expensive as his designer jacket did. Dolefully, he locked eyes with hers. "Miss, any spare change?"

The way you are dressed, you should be giving me *money.* "No. None. Sorry."

His gaze followed hers down to his feet. "Thanks a lot. Bitch," he whispered, walking past her to his next victim, a young woman pushing dark-headed twins in a double-sided stroller.

"True colours. Asshole," Fiona shouted, a warning signal to the young mother. Message received, the woman about-faced, turning the stroller away from the both of them like someone maneuvering a lawn mower around a wide hedge. Undeterred, the man-boy kept walking, his hand now extended toward an older man holding onto a leash as his dog sniffed its way around a tree.

On the very remote chance the old man might know when the next bus was coming, Fiona leaned over the bench. His cigarette, now down to the filter, still hung from his bottom lip. Its ash lay undisturbed on his coat where it had fallen. "Sir, excuse me. Do you know when the next bus is coming?"

For the first time, the old man looked up at her. He spit the butt out of his mouth. "1978. Hey, gotta smoke?"

Swear to God, this city. Deciding it best not to engage further, Fiona turned to look at the dental office window behind her. A big, white, plastic tooth and a big, orange plastic toothbrush, both grinning like Cheshire cats, held a sign that read: "Welcoming new patients." Beside this merry couple, an old, haggard, frumpy Fiona stared back at her. Even with leave-in conditioner, smoother, and humidity-control hair spritzer, in the late February rains, Fiona reminded herself of an unshorn, gray-wooled sheep. She watched as her reflection pulled up the hood of her rain jacket. *Maybe a new raincoat? New shoes? A new outfit? Some hair colour?* Her thoughts interrupted by the sound of squealing brakes behind her, she turned. The old man continued to sit, still staring blankly out onto the traffic of Commercial Drive as he took a cigarette from his coat pocket and, breathing deeply, lit it with his lighter.

As Fiona stepped into her doctor's office, the cloying, medicinal smell hit her. Common to all doctors' offices—as were stethoscopes, weight scales, and disgruntled receptionists—the aroma hung heavy in the air. A spy on a reconnaissance mission, Fiona took a quick look around. Across from her, an older man was ushered into an examination room. He looked frightened, like a prisoner being led from view in one of those old, grainy, black-and-white WWII news clips. She ran over to his now vacant chair, calling out to the receptionist: "Fiona Waters. Dr Chan. 10:10." A seasoned nurse, she knew full well that an empty chair at the doctor's office was a rare occurrence. If it called for sprinting, you sprinted.

Fiona pulled her sweater up over her head and forcefully stuffed it into her backpack. A dishevelled heap of plastic toys, a few under-five spill-proof picture books, a haphazardly folded newspaper, and a stack of parenting magazines crowded the small table beside her. No room. She placed her belongings on her lap.

Fiona took another visual sweep of the waiting room. By the sounds of the rheumy coughs, the moans, and the worried looks of accompanying family members, Fiona could tell she was in for a long haul. Silently, she recited her newest positivity prayer. *I commit to being a grateful and positive person. I look to the universe to share its abundance with me.* It seemed to be working. Day three of her newest foray into positivity and not only did she get a last-minute doctor's appointment, she wasn't leaning up against a wall waiting for her name to be called. Now, if only Dr Chan would sign her stress-leave form. She repeated her prayer. (A person could always use more abundance.)

Her positivity beaming like a flashlight in a darkened wood, Fiona reached into her backpack. She was only three chapters away from finishing her book, *Oryx and Crake*, another doom-filled

Margaret Atwood dystopia. She'd been living with this apocalyptic tale for two months now and was ready for a lighter read. Possibly something along the lines of a true detective or serial killer genre.

"Damn, where is my book?" Forgetting she wasn't in the privacy of her own home, Fiona said this out loud. The two patients flanking her on each side, and maybe even the jaundiced man sitting across from her, looked with trepidation. Fiona knew what those looks meant. Nobody wants to sit near the doctor's office waiting room weirdo.

Her foray into positivity over, Fiona zipped her backpack closed and looked up at the TV mounted high on the wall over the receptionist's head. A distant hum of *The Price is Right* played out from the 24" TV screen.

"Even a dog couldn't hear that," Fiona mumbled, looking around to see if anyone else agreed. Instead, she was met with surreptitious, sideways glances from the two men sitting beside her. The man with jaundice sat staring up at *The Price is Right*, avoiding her gaze. All the other waiting room denizens, earbuds in place, had their heads bent toward their phones.

Bored, Fiona looked down at the table beside her and picked up what was left of the three-day-old newspaper. As always, Vancouver's high housing prices were front and centre. To someone like Fiona just trying to keep up with rent, buying a fixer-upper for one million dollars wasn't a dream, it would be a miracle. Fiona searched through the paper to the classified section. Much thinner than it used to be, the classifieds weren't held in the same regard as they once were. They'd been replaced with the likes of craigslist, Kijiji, or Facebook when seeking employment, a used car, a lost dog, a lover. Fiona turned the page. In bold print, an ad was laid out before her.

Waterview Retirement Village.
Seeking Registered Nurse. Wages to be negotiated.
No solicitations, please. Interested parties send
résumé along with recent references to ad #851116.
Only preferred respondents will be notified. Please
see our website for further details about Waterview
Retirement Village: A new way of being.

She shook her head. When she was young, the elderly went into nursing homes. But now that boomers were the elderly, they moved to retirement living. She could just hear her grandmother: "They're making a silk purse out of a sow's ear, Fiona. Lipstick on a pig."

"Ms Waters. Please come with me," the receptionist called, coming out from behind her desk.

Fiona tucked Section D into her backpack for a second perusal should her request for stress leave not go as planned.

Dr Chan entered the examination room and closed the door. "So what brings you here today?" she asked abruptly, setting her open laptop on the counter.

The bus, Fiona felt like answering to help lighten the mood. Considering Dr Chan's tone of voice, the standing-room-only waiting area, and the fact that the receptionist had gone for lunch, she decided against it. Fiona knew full well that a person in need of a stress leave did not have the upper hand and could not afford to take frivolous chances with levity. Fiona paused. Something she had learned to do at a 'Think Before You Speak' seminar a past employer sent her.

"Well, Dr Chan, lately I've been feeling overwhelmed and tired and I..."

"Everyone is feeling overwhelmed and tired," Dr Chan interrupted.

Fiona noted that Dr Chan was definitely lacking in the empathy department. "I realize societies' pressures affect us all, Dr Chan. I've been nursing now for thirty-five years without taking a break. Except, of course, for my few vacation days each year. It's taking a toll on me. Nursing has never been easy and my current job is causing me unbearable stress. I'm having problems sleeping. I'm overeating. My wine consumption has increased. I have difficulty concentrating."

Humbling oneself before an openly rigid healthcare professional who obviously had her own thoughts about the weariness of the world was humiliating. But Fiona wasn't there for the world. She was there for herself. Fiona needed time. Time to rest. Time to think. Time for her. Time was the only thing that could save her from a nervous breakdown. She could only get that time on a prescribed, paid stress leave. Or by winning a lotto and quitting her job. Sitting up against the wall, doing a quick assessment of her situation (as learned from an 'Assess Your Situation So You Can Get It Right' seminar)—the blood pressure cuff dangling from the holder just to the right of her head and Dr Chan, perched on her stool, looking over at her—it seemed to Fiona her chances for either were about equal.

"You're lucky you've got vacation. Some people in this world never get such an opportunity," Dr Chan answered. "There are times I have had to cancel vacation plans because I have no one to cover for me. I can't just get up and walk away."

Fiona wondered just how her request for a stress leave had become about Dr Chan. However, arguing was not going to help bolster her case. She continued. "I do realize, Dr Chan, that I'm lucky. But after almost three decades working, I need more than a three-week vacation to recuperate. I'm doing the work of two nurses for the pay of one. A poorly paid one, I might add. I take shorter lunch breaks. I leave late, and I still can't catch up on my work. I don't know if I can do it for much longer." Fiona looked down, her eyes searching the floor. (Looking pitiful was one of the tools in her get-a-stress-leave toolbox.) When she glanced up, the look Dr Chan returned was that doctor's look that says they don't believe you but will let you continue as they wait for you to screw up your story. Fiona quickly looked back down at the floor.

"Let's see if there is anything in your lab results."

Blood work results! Finally, they were getting down to something concrete that Dr Chan could zero in on. Sitting there, Fiona hoped the news wasn't devastating but could bolster the case for her stress leave. Something in the way of an easily cured iron deficiency. An-elevated-yet-still-within-normal-range blood sugar. A cloudy urine. A mildly out-of-whack sodium level. All results easily remedied while not signalling imminent death.

"Hmmm," Dr Chan said, looking over at Fiona.

Slowly, Fiona raised her eyes.

"You're as healthy as a horse."

Damn it all! When it came to procuring stress leave, it was never good news when a doctor brought up a cliché that included an animal and its health. Fiona started to think she might need a stress leave to work on getting a stress leave.

Before Dr Chan closed up her computer, Fiona continued. Her voice, now high-pitched, made her sound like someone lost, needing directions to an important appointment they were already late for. "Dr Chan, it's my employer, Dr Wade. He makes my life miserable. I almost think he is being even more disagreeable than normal so that I'll quit and he won't have to give me severance pay. Although, between you and me, I can't see anyone wanting my job."

"Dr Wade? The family practitioner? I know him. Did I know you work for him?"

Do doctors ever listen? "I was sure I told you, Dr Chan. I think you mentioned you went to medical school with his wife. They've recently divorced."

"Actually, I went to medical school with both of them. He and I went out a few times, before I met my husband, of course. If I hadn't met my husband... But I don't recall you mentioning Dr Wade's name before."

Fiona started to think it was better when Dr Chan forgot she worked for Dr Wade.

"Interestingly enough I saw Dr Wade at a seminar recently. Charles told me about his divorce. It sounds like he's hoping to make a few changes to his business model. He told me he wants to turn a new page, gain a fresh perspective. Charles seemed quite positive about it all. Although, he did mention a long-term employee. I guess she's difficult. Do you know her?"

The jerk's discussing me at a cocktail party? It's not like he's making my life all lavender and daffodils. But Fiona had little time to ruminate. With the British Columbia fee-for-service healthcare system, you had ten minutes of care for one problem, and they were already six minutes into it. This meant Fiona had four minutes left to make a case for her stress leave. Included in that was the perfunctory one-minute Dr Chan would take to look down at her watch and start talking about concluding the visit as she closed her computer, got up from her stool, and headed for the door.

"Dr Chan, I think Dr Wade means me."

"Oh..."

Fiona wondered how that was all Dr Chan could say after she had divulged something so private. Then again, if it got her a stress leave...

Swearing, Fiona hit the alarm button and got out of bed. She jammed her left foot into her right slipper. What she wouldn't give for five more minutes. But those five-minute-mores usually turned into ten; into fifteen; into being late, calling a cab, and running into the office only to find Dr Wade's frowny-face staring at her. Her other slipper missing in action, Fiona kicked off the one she was wearing. She looked down at her bed. The jumbled sheets from a restless night's sleep dreaming of a denied stress leave looked like something Houdini had thrown off making one of his grand escapes.

Fiona bent over and, with a wide sweep of her arms, threw the duvet cover over the jumbled sheets. Suddenly, a warm, familiar wetness spread itself along the bottom of her pyjamas. (She called these her oh-no moments.). As clumsily as a contestant in a potato-sack race, Fiona squeezed her legs together and jump-hopped her way to the bathroom. Quickly, she lowered herself onto the cold, white toilet seat. This was part one of her post-menopausal, leaky-bladder routine. Part two was getting up and then sitting back down to make sure her bladder was fully emptied.

No more drops left to squeeze Fiona walked over to the shower. After a long conversation some years earlier with Dr Wade about tardiness and expectations, to save time Fiona had gotten her beauty regime down to ten minutes. She'd taken the routine from a *Cosmopolitan* article: "French Women's Art to Looking Beautiful." Fiona wasn't too sure the regime was working. All she knew was, after ten years, she wasn't about to give up on it now.

First on the list was a cool morning shower, said to invigorate. Invigorate what, Fiona couldn't remember. She held her hand under the shower head waiting for the water to warm. *Who wants a cool shower?* Fiona stepped in and reached for her moisturizing, fragrance-free soap. This was recommended after an episode of dry patches sent her scratching to the dermatologist.

Skin patted to almost dry, her dual-action body lotion promised to fight cellulite while at the same time adding much-needed moisture. A true believer in "more is more," Fiona slathered it on. Then walking over to the vanity, of which, if she were honest, she had little left, Fiona pumped out two squirts of her anti-aging serum. She remembered grimacing when the sales clerk had suggested it for her mature skin. But Fiona, reeled in by its promise of wrinkle-reducing and skin-firming moisturizing with a dewy bloom of youth (jawline only, no jowls included), bought it. These were all miracles a gal could use.

Next, using her fourth fingers to avoid pressure—a gem learned from the same *Cosmopolitan* article, in a gentle, clockwise motion—Fiona applied her eye-firming cream for ten seconds to her outer eye area, starting just under the brow. More than once, Fiona wondered what would happen if she went counter clockwise or stopped before ten seconds. But the article said clockwise for ten, so clockwise for ten it was.

Skin regime finished, Fiona took out her hair products. Too many to count, they owned the bottom shelf of her cabinet. She reached for her hair serum (said to prevent lack-luster hair), a heavy-duty balm to eliminate frizz, and smoother to protect from flat-ironing. Based on her Medusa-like appearance the minute she stepped into the elements, Fiona often wondered if her money might be better used saving for a down payment on a condo. Hair tamed for the moment, Fiona walked back to her bedroom and took her scrubs down from the hook on her closet door. Not one of the few on whom scrubs were flattering, Fiona stepped into the boxy-blue pants. Then pulling the matching, boxy-blue top over her head, she tried to avoid poking her eye out with her name badge, already pinned on to save time. Socks, then white sneakers, and voilà, Fiona was ready for another day in the trenches. Ten hours later, bus rides to and from included, Fiona would do it all again, only in reverse and with too much wine when she got home.

Brice

Out of breath, Brice hurried down the stairs as the SkyTrain signal sounded. Like final call at a theatre performance, there would be no late admissions. Shoving past him two steps at a time, heroic in their efforts to not miss the train, both the young and those with good knees raced by. *Oh, for a gentler time.* Brice slowed. The outcome of his doctor's appointment would be the same whether he was or wasn't on time.

As he rounded the platform, a great swish of air from the departing train hit him in the face, but not before he saw a young boy waving from Brice's favourite SkyTrain seat—the very last one in the very last car overlooking the tracks. Brice waved back as the train sped into the darkness of the tunnel, happy for this one small, shared moment of joy. Sharing moments of joy was one of his most favourite things.

He took a look at his fellow travellers. As far as he was concerned, when it came to trains and train stations, you could never be too careful. He'd read one too many stories of someone being pushed before an oncoming train and no way was he going to be six o'clock news fodder.

"Unidentified middle-aged man dead after disgruntled commuter pushes victim in front of oncoming train. 'I was late for work and that fat slow poke was in my way,' the man shouted to onlookers as he was being handcuffed by police. For more on this breaking story, stay tuned."

Brice found a spot just far enough away from all the other passengers jockeying for position along the platform. As he stood waiting, he looked over at the opposite tunnel wall. Across from the river of tracks hung a sea of young, smiling faces. All of the faces on the posters beamed with promise as they advertised a multitude of educational opportunities. From his alma mater, a young woman with close-cropped, Kool-Aid coloured yellow hair and a blue scarf smiled out from underneath the school insignia. The caption below read: "Find your passion in fashion. I did." Brice laughed at the thought that thirty years before, that was him. Only with blue hair and a pink ascot—attire that could get a person gaybashed. Which it did.

But all that was decades ago. No longer poster material, at fifty-five Brice had a paunch that hung more than slightly over his belt buckle. His five-foot-nine-inch frame which he always considered slightly inadequate, had shrunk to five feet eight-and-a-half inches. What was left of his grey hair with the aid of men's wash-in colour shampoo was now chestnut brown and had been for over a decade. His crow's feet had spread to below his eyes and onto his cheeks. And if he shook his head vigorously, his chin moved along with it.

Finally, the three notes—ding, dang, dong—announced the train's arrival. The train coming to take him from his life before to his life after. The doors opened in front of him. No one getting off, Brice squeezed into the packed train car. He found a crack in the wall of people and grabbed onto a pole as tightly as he could manage. How many people like him, Brice wondered, were taking trips to unhappy times ahead?

Not having brought anything to read and tired of scrolling for celebrity dirt on his phone, Brice walked over to the neatly stacked tower of magazines on the table in the corner of his doctor's waiting room. *The Lancet* not his taste, he picked up a boomer magazine. (Technically a Gen Xer, Brice was just happy to have something to read.) One headline caught his eye: "How to Prevent Aging—the Newest in Non-Surgical Face Lifts." Brice started flipping through the magazine. *For Pete's sake, there are so many ads in here, I may need Google Maps to find the article.* Continuing his search, one ad caught his eye.

Waterview Retirement Village.
A community within a community offering gourmet meals, light housekeeping services, fitness facilities, and so much more. Retirement at its best, Waterview Retirement Village gives you the freedom and independence to reach your dreams. We are an independent to full-care living facility.
Visit our website below.

Surely, there couldn't be all that many dreams left by the time you needed full nursing care? Maybe a dream that your meal was served hot. Or that you could manage a good bowel movement every morning. Maybe even a dream for a new walker. The kind you could sit on when you were tired. Maybe to make it cheery you could attach a few rainbow-coloured streamers to the handles.

Inwardly Brice fumed. The ad had to have been written by some bright-future, politically correct, millennial marketer who couldn't visualize for even a nanosecond that one day they might be in the same position. Did they think people were that stupid? Trying to make a nursing home sound like a great new area of town? Instead of what it really was—a place where you're left lined up before the shared flat screen in the lobby, drooling away in your high-backed wheelchair, stuck watching some TV show you didn't care for while you waited for the aide to take you to the bathroom for a pee or put you down for the night.

Maybe if it sounded better? Something like Waterview Retirement Village. Only pronounced, Ville-ah-jj, emphasis on the ah. Anyone could tell Waterview Retirement Ville-ah-jj was so much more exotic and not quite so one-foot-closer-to-the-grave sounding. So, having some big decisions to make, Brice gave a loud cough as he ripped the page from the magazine. As soon as he did this, out from behind her black dollar store glasses, the receptionist sitting upright in her chair glared at him. From past experience Brice knew a person coughing in a doctor's office waiting room did not endear one to the receptionist. He watched her as she watched him. Still not on a first-name basis, he'd known Ms Winworth for more than a decade now. Brice's brain could be coming through his left nostril and would he find an ounce of sympathy in her fixed, steely-blue eyes? Not a chance. A little sympathy would have been welcomed too. Any fool knows that when your family doctor calls you in three days after you've seen a specialist, you're either dying or about to die.

"Sir, I can't discuss this over the phone. Dr Kapolian has to talk to you. No, he can't talk to you over the phone either. He needs to see you in person."

Ms Winworth may not like a cougher, but Brice had to give her her due. She was an expert. She anticipated the answer before you came up with the question. It gave him a certain level of comfort knowing everyone was treated the same way. No matter whether you had a case of contact dermatitis or flesh-eating disease, there were no favourites. Naturally, he had been more than a little worried when she called him yesterday. There was an outside chance his rosacea cream refill was up. But deep down Brice knew within his inner being what was wrong. He could only pray that the specialist and Dr Google had made a mistake. That his symptoms were because of some strange new virus that would eventually go away.

A virus could explain a lot of things. A runny nose. Why you couldn't lift your left arm. The reason your computer crashed. While you had them, viruses were troubling, and they might take time to get rid of but eventually they went away. Amyotrophic lateral sclerosis (ALS), on the other hand, which is what Brice suspected, not only stuck around to the end, it was the end.

Uncle Jim on his dad's side had died of ALS. Brice was only seven when he saw his dear uncle for the last time. The whole family had gone to visit Uncle Jim, who had moved back home to the farm with his mother after his wife left when she found out what she was in for. Brice could still see his grandmother as she looked the day his family drove up the driveway in their third-hand, green, wood-panelled station wagon. She stood on the front porch waiting to greet them. Standing there, thin and angular, worry had carved her face into an emblem of pain and long-suffering. To a young boy, she seemed distant and formidable. Even now, Brice felt profound sadness thinking of what she must have been going through. His grandmother had only been trying to do her best for his Uncle Jim, her son. Of course, reflecting back on that day was difficult for Brice. It wasn't easy seeing yourself as an unkind child. But how had that day become his fault? He'd expected to see his beloved uncle as he always had been. Not what he had become.

Because of Uncle Jim, family visits to the farm had always been full of laughter and knock-knock jokes and discoveries like wasp nests and the sound of frogs singing. Time spent with his uncle was better than any amusement park ride. Uncle Jim would take Brice by an arm and a leg and twirl him around and up and down, all the while mimicking the hum of an airplane. Reality suspended, Uncle Jim as his pilot, Brice became the most important passenger in his own private plane. That was the magic of his uncle. He was all make-believe and imagination, unlike his brother, Brice's father. And on that long-ago sunny summer day, not seeing his uncle on the doorstop, Brice, with outstretched arms anticipating his embrace, ran through the farmhouse calling out: "Uncle Jim. Uncle Jim."

What he found instead was a stranger beside the kitchen window, slumped over in a wheelchair, a strap cinching him to the chair. Brice remembered the river of spittle running down the stranger's slackened face. Where was Uncle Jim? Brice had been about to turn and run from the room crying. That was until his father came from behind, placing his hands on Brice's shoulders. Not for comfort. There was never any comfort. The brick-like weight was to keep him there.

"Brice, give your uncle a kiss," his father commanded. With horror, Brice watched as this new Uncle Jim mumbled something Brice couldn't understand.

What Brice did understand was his grandmother translating how happy uncle Jim was to see them all. Then Brice did something he had shoved away deep into his box of forever sorries. He ran into his mother's arms, crying to go home, looking to be saved. Instead, his mother told him he was a rude little boy. That if he wasn't going to behave, he could go sit in the car and wait. But already, at seven, Brice knew that only meant punishment was delayed until after he got home. So he stayed.

Even now, Brice could never understand how they could have expected anything else. They hadn't prepared him or his sister Marcia for that visit. Hadn't told them about the changes in their uncle. Hadn't warned them. And even if they had, he and his sister were too young to understand that ALS was the disease. ALS was not their uncle.

Scared silent the rest of that afternoon, Brice remembered wondering if he was the only one who saw what was happening. How his uncle's head bobbed uncontrollably. How Uncle Jim struggled to cough. How the saliva spilled from his mouth and ran down his bib. Sitting there in the kitchen that day, Brice listened to the adults discussing the next steps, when the time came. Whatever the next steps and the time came meant. That difficult day was the last time he saw his uncle, Brice's parents deciding it was better not to take him or his sister Marcia again. Sadly, after that day his parents, too, rarely visited. Poor Uncle Jim. Not only had he been abandoned by his health, he'd been abandoned by his family.

Now it was Brice's turn. There would be no one to wipe his mouth. Or anything else for that matter. Holding his backpack closer, he waited. He couldn't lose that advertisement.

Ushering Brice into the room, Dr Kapolian shut the door to his office. "Please take a chair."

Brice had only been in this room once before. Years before when Peter, his husband, had received his cancer diagnosis. As far as Brice knew, the doctor's personal office was a room most patients never got to visit. Unless there was bad news.

Brice's memory of the room was much the same as what he now saw. The large, black-rimmed clock remained on the wall over the sink to Brice's right. The second hand moved in a silent staccato along with Brice's heartbeat. To the left, the white wall had a single window. It was fitted with small-slatted, white, wooden Venetian blinds that could be closed should the sunlight prove too much. Behind Dr Kapolian's desk, four diplomas and two certificates centred on the wall affirmed that, yes, he was indeed a doctor and with it came the unspoken suggestion that he knew what he was doing and not to worry. Brice laughed to himself. *Maybe next time I'll bring along my two-year diploma in fashion design school.*

What were missing were any intimate photos of family. No pictures of skiing trips with friends or fish dangling from a pole. Nothing to show Dr Kapolian had a life outside work. Brice looked back at the window and watched as a grey-blue pigeon pecked at the sill and, finding nothing there, flew off.

Each step was heavy with worry as Brice moved toward the offered chair. Brice sat down. Dr Kapolian came over. He was wearing his usual uniform of a pressed white lab coat over a white shirt, black tie with an exact Windsor knot, and black pants. He sat down in his large, black, leather chair behind his large, lacquered, black desk. There was no smile on his face, only solemn determination. The space dividing them seemed as wide and far apart as one of those cracks mountaineers fall into that they aren't able to climb out of; their vulture-picked bones found decades later by a new generation of climbers better equipped for difficult terrain.

"Brice, I'm afraid it's not good news."

If he's afraid, what am I? Brice looked down at his hands. They were shaking. From what? Nerves? Cold? The disease?

"With your self-report of decreased ability to hold onto things, your voice sounding deeper and strained, along with your uncle's history of ALS, as you know, I referred you to a neurologist, Dr Samuels. Dr Samuels did a physical examination and ordered electromyography. That test measures the electrical conduction of your nerves and the electrical conduction of your muscles." Dr Kapolian paused and took a deep breath. "Brice, I'm sorry to tell you this. The results show you've got Amyotrophic Lateral Sclerosis or ALS. You might also know it as Lou Gehrig's disease. Based on your history, yours is likely inherited or Familial Amyotrophic Lateral Sclerosis or FALS. FALS occurs in 5% to 10% of cases. But your diagnosis seems even more rare because it may have come from your uncle and not a parent. So we aren't certain if you have ALS or FALS. Either way, it isn't a good diagnosis."

The man never did know how to segue between saying hello and filling you in on impending doom. Dr Kapolian just let fly with the bad news, handed you more test requisitions, offered you a sleeping pill, and sent you on your way. It was the same thing when Peter was diagnosed with pancreatic cancer six years ago. Except Brice had been there when Peter got his diagnosis. Now Peter was gone. Aside from his sister Marcia, Brice was alone, and he doubted Marcia would be much help. She lived thousands of miles away.

But deep down, Brice had known, even before his examination by the specialist, that his difficulty gripping his coffee cup handle meant something wasn't right. He felt like throwing up. His life as he knew it was over. He told himself not to cry. He didn't want Dr Kapolian resorting to platitudes and false reassurances.

"You know, Brice, a diagnosis of FALS or ALS is eventually terminal." Dr Kapolian came over and sat on the corner of his desk, across from Brice.

Just how many times a week does this man have to give devastating news to a patient? No wonder he sounds like someone reading from the manual How to Tell a Patient Devastating News in Under Five Minutes.

"Researchers are working on a cure, but so far there's been little success. Good news, the ice bucket campaign a few years back raised a lot of money and awareness for ALS. But there's still a long way to go before researchers find a cure. You say you've been feeling off for about a year. So with your self-report, along with the results of Dr Samuel's examinations, if we can call it the normal trajectory of ALS, it looks as if you have at most between three to five years of living left. As I said, there is no cure. However, there are things to assist you with living quite well with the disease. This is not easy to discuss, I know. But as ALS progresses, you will lose your bodily functions. Eventually, you will require total care. Know that together we will come up with a plan for you as you progress. Today I'm giving you a prescription for some medication. It can be helpful with the symptoms if started early on, and this is early on. Brice, I know all this is difficult to hear. But you need to know the truth so you can start planning for the future."

Brice sat silently, stunned by the reality of Dr Kapolian's words. He'd considered ALS, but to hear his diagnosis made it real. Real was not the place Brice wanted to be. What he wanted was for it to not be ALS. To not be anything. To have his Peter back. To reverse time. What was he going to do?

Brice woke up to disco music playing from the radio, tuned to easy listening. Just exactly when disco had become easy listening, Brice wasn't sure. He was just happy there was a station still playing it. The music brought back memories of being underage, sneaking into gay bars, loving the glitter, and finding his true self. As the pre-programmed coffee aroma drifted up to his nose, an enticement, Brice willed himself out of bed. *At least I can still get up on my own.* Walking barefoot to the bathroom, he hoped to avoid a repeat of yesterday morning's trip over his slipper. Brice stopped to look at the professionally framed photographs hanging in the hallway.

"We'll make a collage of ourselves together," Peter had said, hammering a nail into the wall as another nail dangled from the side of his mouth. The first photo was of them sitting on a red-and-white checkered blanket at Second Beach, a bottle of red and a picnic basket before them. They were celebrating their first anniversary as husband and husband. In the next photograph, they were dressed up as scary clowns riding the Stanley Park Halloween train. Then, later that year (because one could never get enough of the Stanley Park train), Santa Peter and Elf Brice took another turn around the park on the Christmas train. Beside that photo, one from New Year's Eve—of them kissing under a clock reading 11:47. (A picture at midnight cost $100 more.) For their only venture to the Maritimes, a tripod picture of the two of them on the rocks at Peggy's Cove commemorated their visit. Last, a headshot of Peter on the cover of *Time's* "Man of the Year" issue. Brice had a computer friend do it up as a joke, but it looked so good they hung it on the wall.

"You look like a movie star," Brice said each time he looked at it, both before Peter's death and after it.

"Time to take some of those down, don't you think?" This from his sister Marcia, one painfully long visit after Peter's death. "It's like a gay shrine in here."

"There can never be too many Peter pictures," Brice replied, hanging up the Peggy's Cove picture before she left.

His hip ached. The large bruise on his left outer thigh, now dark red, had grown since his fall the day before. Lifting the toilet seat, Brice aimed his penis at the centre of the bowl. This was his newest test for—for what exactly? Coordination? Concentration? Muscle strength? The penis wasn't even a muscle. Was it?

Bladder emptied, proud there was no urine on the rim or floor, he walked over to the shower. After the water warmed to just right, he got in. *Look at me, Baldylocks and the Three Bears*. Laughing, he reached for his shampoo. In a circular motion, he washed his hair and the bald spot at the crown. *Good thing I can't see it. I'm sure that thing is spreading like the plague.* Then, loofah and body wash in hand, he started scrubbing. How many mornings were left before he'd need help bathing?

He looked down and soaped up his flaccid penis. It reminded him of an earthworm reaching out of the dark, dry earth searching for rain. No longer shared with others, he rubbed up and down the shaft with his loofah. Each movement was faster than the one before as his tears joined the water raining from the shower head. Peter.

"Such a fabulous way to start the day," Peter would joke after one of their morning shower quickies. After Peter's cancer spread, those morning showers had turned into Peter sitting on a plastic bath chair, Brice washing him.

He cried harder. *For God's sake, get on with this before your dick lets you down.*

Finished, he turned off the water and reached for his Bellagio beach towel hanging over the bathtub. He and Peter had spent their last real holiday together in Las Vegas. A bargain package of two nights at Circus Circus and economy airfare out of Seattle was all they could afford. But Peter, knowing Brice really wanted to do it up at the Bellagio, bought him this beach towel.

"Ain't life grand? Besides, no one really has to know we didn't stay there." Peter had laughed. And it *had* been grand and good and happy and full of love. Then Peter got sick later that year and died the next. It had all been so fast—no time for Brice to catch his breath.

One last look in the mirror—ready, set, go. Ready, except for what he was going to tell his co-workers. Not that it was any of their business. But since the eighties, whenever a gay man had a medical appointment or took a leave, everyone assumed it had something to do with HIV. Not that ALS was any picnic.

Brice got to the bus stop with no trips over his feet. *Maybe that trip over my slipper yesterday was just that. A trip over my slipper.* Before his ALS symptoms, neuron messages were something he hadn't thought about since grade ten biology. Or was that chemistry? Now, in his case, the messages were being sent, they just didn't always arrive. The #5 bus pulled up to the stop and the doors opened. He got on and took a seat.

Brice loved every little thing about his job dressing windows in the heart of downtown Vancouver. His canvas was the space, glass, lights, and high ceilings. The clothing was his subject. The mannequins, his muse. The customers, his audience. Each season, there was something new and exciting from the fashion houses of Paris, Milan, London, Seoul. His job was to bring those fashions to life in Vancouver—to let people see themselves as real-life fashionistas. Today, standing before the store with his disability letter in his leather satchel, looking at what was most likely his last window, Brice felt pride. The sales of designer men's shirts had gone up 10%. The big boss linked the purchasing surge to Brice's fabulously dressed mannequins in the store window. And they were all fabulously dressed, each taking on their own persona. Not easy when you have the same white, bald head with the same white, blank face and the same white, square body shape to work with.

He'd managed to drag a black mannequin out from the back of the storage closet. "This one usually only sees the light of day during black history month," he told his department manager,

George, as he pulled it along the floor toward the featured window. "Didn't you hear? The world is made up of more than white men. That goes for mannequins too. Jonathon here" —Brice gestured to the black mannequin he'd hoisted into the window box— "needs to come out more. P.S., he's gay. Samuel over there" —Brice pointed to a white mannequin wearing a shocking orange wig and a pink T-shirt— "he's bisexual."

Oh, how Brice could work miracles with a window.

He looked down at his watch. Fifteen minutes until his appointment with George. Brice walked to the store's front entrance. A young man walking ahead of him opened the heavy, glass door and swung it open wide. Brice hurried in behind him. He took the escalator up to the fifth floor.

"Hi, Brice. Come on in. I hope everything's OK with you. Your voice sounded kinda ominous on the phone."

"Ominous? I didn't mean it to be."

George reached over and took the crisp, white envelope Brice offered him. "What's this? I hope it's not your resignation. You're the best window designer out there."

"No, not that. I need to take a leave. That's my disability form all filled in and signed by my doctor."

George carefully opened the letter. "I'm just giving it a quick glance but it looks fine. As you know, I can't ask what's wrong, but Brice, please, if you need anything, don't hesitate to call. I mean it. I'll do my best to help. You're a valued employee."

"Thanks, George."

Outside the office door, Brice dabbed at his eyes with his designer kerchief. Best to leave with some dignity before any other staff came by and he needed to explain things.

Too upset to walk home with his usual jaunty step, Brice caught the bus. Diet be damned. He intended to eat the rest of the flourless chocolate cake he'd bought the day before, after his talk with Dr Kapolian. In fact, his entire plan was to eat his way through every last fattening and cholesterol-laden food known to humanity, which might just be the only bright side to dying. Then, after his gorge and some Bachelorette, Brice would go to bed. Alone. Again. Thinking of his Peter and their life together. Happy memories from times past. A way to divert his thoughts from this awful thing lurking in the dark corners of his mind.

Adelina

Cold and rainy, March had come in like a lion. Adelina sat on the large, upholstered vinyl chair consuming her bony five-foot-four-inch frame. Her shoulders hunched, she yawned quietly through closed lips as the corners of her mouth pulled down in a grimace. Adelina looked down at her dry, cracked, brown hands. She'd forgotten her hand cream downstairs in the housekeeping department. Cracked open areas were not good with her diabetes. Luckily, she had had enough time to brush her teeth and pull her hair into a tighter knot at the crown. Adelina pulled at her coat, trying to hide her dirt-stained clothes. It was hard to look presentable after working all night cleaning.

As though she were a sky observer watching an eclipse of the sun when cautioned not to, Adelina looked out the big picture windows of Dr Lovell's office at the rising sun. She knew from cleaning them that the view included three bridges and the downtown area. Hopefully, March's end would be like a lamb and the weather would be good. The cool, grey, wet days of early March had such a depressing effect on people.

Why am I still here, God? I need to go home to bed. She thought back to her talk with Dr Lovell the night before.

"I'd like to have a conversation with you. Not now. I realize you need to start working and I have to get home. It's been a long day in the operating room. How's the morning, before I see my follow-up appointments? I promise I won't keep you long."

But she knew that no one talked to the cleaning staff unless there was a problem. She needed to get home. She hadn't called her husband Don to let him know she'd be late from work after her night shift. There was no point. His pain, the great overseer, determined his schedule. At this hour, Don might be sleeping, or he might be watching TV. Either way, a call would not be welcomed.

Looking around, Adelina wondered if all the patients filling the waiting room were cosmetic or if any of them had real problems. The kinds of problems she had. The kind surgery couldn't fix.

Something must be going on for Dr Lovell to ask her to stay late. He'd never done this before. Plus, Joni, her cleaning partner, kept hinting there was going to be a shake-up. Joni always seemed to know when things were happening at work. Like when Sheila had been signing in, then leaving. Joni had known Sheila was getting fired before Sheila had.

Getting their carts ready the week before, Joni, with a conspiratorial whisper, had handed Adelina the job posting for Waterview Retirement Village. "They're hiring. I'd look into it myself, but I'm staying put no matter what's happening around here. Night shift fits with my family."

Adelina knew this wasn't true. Joni's husband had left her more than five years ago, and she had no kids. What Joni did have was a drinking problem. Working nights kept her out of trouble. Adelina prayed every day for God to keep Joni strong. She knew too well from her own husband what kind of problems drinking led to.

But if there was trouble brewing, a change of employment might be nice. Plus, Waterview offered benefits. Benefits were rare these days, let alone good ones. With the cost of both of their medications, and Don's disability barely covering half the rent, help paying for their drugs would be one less worry. For Joni to leave Office Cleaning Services, it would have to be for a big pay increase. They both knew that was not going to happen. No one pays big for cleaners.

Adelina liked working with Joni. She'd been with Office Cleaning Services for a good five years before Adelina started working there eleven years ago. Slowly, they had gotten to know each other on their nightly rides from the basement up to the fourth floor, then back down again when their shift was over each morning. The start of their friendship had been like picking away at the fuzz on a sweater. Adelina had been assigned to Dr Lovell's plastic surgery and cosmetic procedures services clinic. Joni was responsible for Dr Mark and Dr Markham's rectal surgery and hemorrhoid banding procedures clinic. Each doctor's office took up a full wing. Both had six examination rooms to clean, three bathrooms, two large procedure rooms and a reception area.

"And a partridge in a pear tree." This from under Joni's breath whenever they had to list their duties for work questionnaires. These past few months, there had been more work surveys handed out than anyone could remember. It was causing gossip amongst the cleaners. Everyone knew the contract was up.

Adelina had been there for about three years when she and Joni really got to know each other. Joni had come over to Dr Lovell's to ask Adelina for help. One of the bathrooms was a big mess. The toilet was clogged with wads of toilet paper; there was urine all over the floor and excrement covered the toilet seat. Joni said she should put a camera in there to see what kind of animal would do such a thing. But that was just talk. Such an act would get them fired. And that was how they started working both offices together. Adelina loved Joni's company and the help. That extra pair of hands, lifting heavy desks and chairs while the other vacuumed, saved their backs. Pete, their boss, didn't know they did this. Joni was always saying the company liked to keep everyone separate so the cleaners couldn't organize. That was the thing with Joni— she had lots of conspiracy theories. Lately, Adelina was starting to think she was right.

The man sitting across from Adelina with the bandage on the bridge of his nose, his eyes blackened from bruising, started to mumble. Something about pay parking and his time and deducting his $200-an-hour salary from the cost of his surgery. How entitled was that man, thinking he didn't have to wait like everyone else? Saying such a thing just loud enough to be heard would not make things go any faster. Adelina knew that when it came time to talk to the doctor, he'd be all smiles. She held back another yawn. All she wanted to do was to crawl into bed before she had to get up later this evening and start all over again. That man across from her was just starting his day. He'd mumble a lot louder if he were in her shoes.

Adelina looked down at her feet. *At least I have time to think.* Time for herself was one thing she rarely had these days. That was funny. No time for time. She'd have to tell Joni that one tonight at work.

Not many people liked working the night shift. Adelina did. Not that she had a choice. It was nights or nothing. But Adelina found she liked the slower pace and that no one was looking over her shoulder, telling her what to do. Plus, working nights brought people close. It had been that way with Joni anyway. Maybe because she didn't get to socialize as much with old friends, them being on day hours; instead, she shared the night saying things to her co-worker she wouldn't say to anyone else. Not even to Don. Besides, Don was not the kind of man you told things to. Not unless you wanted to be told to shut up or to get hit. Anyway, it was very considerate of Joni to confide in her about the Waterview job. It showed how much she trusted Adelina. The staff all knew that if word got out you were looking at another job, you'd be fired. Their job was not a good job, but all the staff needed it.

Looking out the window, she saw a seagull flying high up in the bright sunshine. Adelina thought of the man who flew too close to the sun. Someone or something was always there to burn you. Maybe this Waterview really was a good employer. It would be nice to work at a place that treated her well, where she didn't have to throw in ten dollars for food and party favours at the annual Christmas party and summer barbeque.

Whenever Adelina went to one of the two annual events, Joni said the same thing. "Office Cleaning Services has to be making a profit from these parties. Otherwise, they wouldn't do it." Most of the time they served Canadian Chinese food or hamburgers. At the end of the night everyone put their shiny neon hats, novelty beads, and metallic rainbow noisemakers into a big black plastic bag to reuse.

At the last Christmas's party, Joe had blown into one. It was so dry with age that no sound came out. No way would Adelina ever do that. Everything had to be full of germs. That was another Joni joke. "The only free thing they give us for Christmas is germs." Plus, ten dollars was a lot of money when you were only making eighteen an hour. But Adelina went anyway. She liked a party. There were so few in her life. And she enjoyed seeing her coworkers outside of work. Everyone was so different away from the job.

Adelina looked at the clock. Why did Dr Lovell think he could ask her to stay without getting paid for her time? Maybe he had found out she and Joni spent their breaks in his office. Adelina would look out at the city lights glittering in the dark of the night and feel she was part of something big. Not that she or Joni touched anything. They just sat in his big comfy chairs, looking out the window, eating their sandwiches and talking.

"It doesn't matter if we make a mess," Joni would say whenever Adelina had doubts about sitting there. "We're cleaning it anyway."

Joni said a corner office showed dominance and power. Maybe making her wait was Dr Lovell's way of showing his dominance and power. Judging by the number of patients waiting to be seen that morning, it was no wonder he could afford such a grand space.

"Mr Bell." A nurse receptionist with overfilled lips, wearing a bright, white, stiff lab coat over black scrubs, called out to the man with the nose bandage. Getting up, the man was all smiles and nods just like Adelina knew he'd be. As for her, if she wasn't called soon, she'd fall asleep in her chair. But Adelina knew she wouldn't leave. When you were on the bottom rung of life's ladder, you stayed there until someone decided to climb over you or put you away in the shed.

"Adelina." A second nurse receptionist in a matching bright, white, stiff lab coat and black scrubs called. Adelina was led to one of the assessment rooms she and Joni had cleaned a couple of hours before. Adelina looked around the room. All of it sparkled, even the faucets. Their work was good. That was for sure.

"Thank you for agreeing to stay." Dr Lovell made it sound like she had a choice. "I know you must be tired."

Adelina knew her rights. She should be getting paid for her time. But she knew it wouldn't get mentioned. It seemed to her that those making the most money begrudged a few dollars to those making the least.

"Adelina," Dr Lovell started again in a heartfelt tone. According to Joni, nothing good ever came when your name was said in a heartfelt tone. "All the doctors in this building are very satisfied with Office Cleaning Services. Personally, I am very pleased with the work you, as an individual, do keeping my office in such great shape." Adelina waited. "But we, that is, the doctors in the building, as a group, are facing financial challenges this year. We need to make changes to our operations."

Adelina wondered why Dr Lovell was telling her this. In the office hierarchy, she was a nobody. Already, this was the longest he had ever spoken to her. When they did speak, it was only in passing when he came in early to see patients. Those times he filled up the garbage cans she had already emptied with dirty bandages, expecting her to empty them again. That was the thing with privatization. His extra requests were not part of the contract. Joni said he was a weasel for making her do these extras when she should be heading home.

"Changes, Dr Lovell?" Adelina said, Joni's words making her

think of a weasel dressed in a bright, white lab coat.

"We need to cut costs. The cleaning budget is one of those cost-saving measures the other doctors and I have been looking at." He said this, looking down, his index finger running down a book on his desk. Adelina had wiped it down enough to know it was his day scheduler.

"How, Dr Lovell?"

"I am sure you know the contract is coming to a close with your current employer. We are negotiating a deal with another company. Bare facts, the new company costs less and offers the same service."

It must have been her extreme tiredness that had her dropping her guard, giving her the courage to speak back to him. "Dr Lovell, we work so hard. We do it for your patients so they don't catch ill. I don't understand how another company can clean the way we do for less. It's not possible."

"Well Adelina, it's possible and it's happening. I have asked that you be the first person offered your old job. If you want it, that is."

Old job. *How can it be old when I am still working at it?* "If I can keep my old job, Dr Lovell, then what exactly is changing?"

"That would be a conversation for you with the new company. It's my understanding from our discussions that your pay will be much the same. However, there will be fewer workers."

"Why are you telling me this, Dr Lovell?" Her boldness that morning kept surprising her.

Looking back down, he slid his finger to a stop on the page. "I really have to get going, Adelina. I know I can trust you not to say anything until your employer informs the rest of the staff that the contract is not being renewed. I wanted to personally let you know how much I value your work. I'd like you to stay, but I understand if you don't."

"Thank you, Dr Lovell."

Making her way to the bus, Adelina thought about the ad for Waterview Retirement Village. She needed to work. Don's disability check alone would not support the two of them. Maybe when Joni heard this news, she would reconsider and apply too. Then they could still be together.

Only one hour later than her usual bus ride home, and already it was standing room only. Grabbing onto the overhead strap, Adelina stood, her legs throbbing. She felt like a hanging meat carcass going to market. Adelina knew there would be no vacant seats until, like wasps being driven from the hive, the bus emptied at Commercial Drive. Adelina's thoughts tossed about. How would she be able to keep such a heavy secret from Joni and the others?

Finally home, Adelina bent her tired back to put the key in the apartment lock. Suddenly the door opened, knocking her off balance.

"I've been waiting for my breakfast." Don stood staring at her with his blue tired eyes, his greying sandy-brown hair dishevelled. He reminded her of an expectant child waiting for his mother's return. Adelina wondered what it would be like to have breakfast waiting for her when she got home.

She headed to their small, time-worn kitchen. It had been at least five years since it was painted. Any requests to the landlord usually resulted in a rent increase, so Adelina remained silent.

"The usual?" Adelina stooped to get the bread from the cupboard.

"No, I don't feel like peanut butter and toast anymore. Maybe if you got home earlier. Now I feel like two eggs, two bacon, two toast, and coffee. Call me when it's ready."

Reaching for the eggs, Adelina wasn't upset that Don hadn't bothered to ask her why she was late. She'd tell him about the changes to her job when she knew more. Right now, explaining would cause him too much anxiety and take her too much energy. Energy she didn't have.

Not enough eggs for her, she ate her bacon and toast, half listening to Don talking about the infomercials he'd watched late into the night. "You should see the crap some people come up with and what people buy. I should invent something and make some big money."

At times like these, Adelina felt like asking Don, "If you could do better, why don't you?" Instead, he just sat there talking and talking. It never seemed to occur to him that while he watched TV into the night, she was hard at work breaking her back.

"...and then CSI, well I'd seen that one before so..."

Adelina sent a quick prayer up to God to give her patience. Joni kept saying Don was lucky Adelina hadn't left. But after thirty-seven years together, how could she? It wasn't Don's fault he got injured on the job and was left in chronic pain and couldn't work. Adelina knew it was hard on him to be unable to provide for his family. Sometimes when things got really bad, Adelina did have fleeting thoughts about leaving him. But where would she go? She'd never been on her own before. And there were her wedding vows—for better or worse, said before God. And even if the scale too often balanced on worse, she would be breaking her promise to God.

"Then I fell asleep on the couch and woke up when I heard you making noise at the door. It's a good thing you came home. I was hungry." Don said, his mouth full as he took his last bit of bread and wiped up his plate with it.

Breakfast over, like soldiers, they each took their stations. Don to the couch, his pistol the remote. Adelina to their galley kitchen, her bulletproof vest an apron. Looking over at Don, engrossed in the TV, she sent a prayer of thanks to God. She'd have their one bedroom to herself. Hopefully that would translate into her getting a good sleep. With all that was on her mind, she wasn't sure.

As Adelina loaded the small, apartment-sized dishwasher, her thoughts turned to her childhood. With God's grace, she'd made as good a life for herself as she could. And even though she had secretly dreamed of going to college, obtaining a post-secondary education had been as far away from her as touching the moon. Her parents, immigrants of colour from Jamaica, had their own problems. Professionals back home, coming to Canada hadn't been easy for them. Too many times, the job was gone when they showed up for the interview. Or the better apartment was suddenly taken when her parents came to see it. They both ended up working two low-paying jobs each to make ends meet. With all their struggles, Adelina felt she owed it to them to help out. And that was what she had done—finished school and started working. In those times, a grade twelve education was more than good enough to land a well-paying job—the hospital cafeteria where she had initially worked paid a living wage. Years later, neither was true. Now, her family lived in Alberta, and everyone was doing fine. Everyone but her.

Adelina stepped into the shower to wash away the filth of the night's work. Soon enough, with the new contract, there would be double the dirt, double the work, double the tiredness. Adelina headed to the bed and knelt beside it. She prayed to God, giving thanks for all the blessings in her life. Lately, it seemed as if the devil was taking scissors and cutting up her list of good things.

In bed, the covers over her, the blinds lowered, ear plugs squeezed into both ears, Adelina dreamt the dreams of the troubled.

Fiona

At the door, Fiona did her usual review. As far as she knew, nothing warranted receiving another talking to by Dr Wade. All month long she'd been the essence of politeness, had shown unlimited patience, had been extra nice to Mr Charles. Mr Charles being the reason she'd been hauled into the office two months before. Exasperated after his fifth call to book an appointment for his little boy's measles shots, Fiona had told him he had the wrong number. Flipping through charts behind her, Dr Wade overheard. On the face of it, Fiona's response sounded like someone playing a mean trick. But Mr Charles's fully-vaccinated son, now forty-six, was living in the U.K. Secretly, Fiona wondered if Mrs Charles had given him the office number to keep him occupied. Fiona understood. Her own mother had been worn down caring for Fiona's father before he died from dementia.

Dr Wade, however, would hear none of it. "Fiona, please answer the phone respectfully to everyone. I don't think I need to tell you that a respectful manner does not include lying to our patients." Dr Wade's look as he said this was either one of condescension or fatigue; Fiona couldn't tell which. But it wasn't Dr Wade trying to assist patients waiting at the desk, faxing off referrals, and answering the office phone—all at the same time. So, the next time Mr Charles called, Fiona transferred the call to Dr Wade. As far as Fiona knew, her probation for that had expired.

Fiona knocked, then entered Dr Wade's office after his cursory, "Open."

Always in a hurry, Dr Wade usually wasted no time telling Fiona what she'd done wrong, what she needed to do to fix it, and how long her probation would be. But today was different. Today he was standing by the window, staring out like a nervous teenager waiting for their prom date to show. Fiona wasn't sure what to make of this. The office was on the second floor overlooking the dumpster. Not the best view of the city.

Sitting down in her usual get-a-talking-to-seat, she took a deep breath into her lungs and then held it for five seconds. Slowly she let the flow of air out, her lips pursed (but not too pursed— she didn't want Dr Wade thinking she had a respiratory problem that might trigger a price increase in the health plan). Usually, deep breathing exercises made Fiona dizzy, but since deep breathing was advised at every stress-reducing seminar Fiona had ever attended, she kept going. They even gave examples: If a bear was about to attack you, if a thief was stealing your bike, if a pervert was feeling up your bum on the SkyTrain. Let the good air in. Hold. Let the bad air out. Then either play dead, shout, or run.

But it was when Dr Wade turned toward her to say something and instead looked over her head at the wall behind her that almost got Fiona hyperventilating. Finally, Dr Wade interrupted the heavy silence. "Fiona, I've made a big decision. I'm closing my practice and joining the Cosmetic Wellness Centre."

Fiona stopped deep breathing. It wouldn't be good to pass out. She might miss something.

Then, not saying anything more, he just stood there. Fiona wondered if he was expecting her to say something. Closing his practice was something Fiona had never envisioned. She moved in closer, tilting her face slightly as if to say, please go on. This strategy allowed her to gather her thoughts while maintaining a look of interest. A technique Fiona had learned at one of the communications workshops she'd been sent to by a former employer. The forward lean let the speaker know the listener was, in fact, listening. For added effect, Fiona started moving her head up and down. At the workshop, Fiona had thought this technique was a load of bunk. But now sitting in Dr Wade's office, shocked, she found herself with her head angled, nodding like a drunk at last call.

"Since my divorce, I've changed," Dr Wade said, coming over to his chair behind his desk and sitting down across from Fiona.

To Fiona, Dr Wade seemed much the same as he always had, which is why she secretly supported his wife in the divorce. But wanting to show she was engaged in the conversation, Fiona focused her eyes on his. Or at least she tried to focus her eyes on his. Fiona soon realized that tilting her head and nodding while trying to fix her eyes took some practice.

As Dr Wade kept talking, even though she had something to say, Fiona didn't interrupt. This valuable technique of attending the speaker by not interrupting came from the second anger management seminar Dr Wade made her take after she had failed the first one. And so far, it seemed to be working. That is, if Dr Wade's non-stop talking was any indication that her attentive listening skills were working. The only trick left in her arsenal was a gentle touch on the shoulder. This technique was one Fiona placed in the "For Use Only in Extreme Situations" category. Like, God forbid, Dr Wade started crying.

"Fiona, I've been a family doctor now for twenty years. My candle has finally burnt itself out. I have nothing left in the tank to give my patients. Trying to help people with all their sad stories—it's endless. Rarely do I get to see happy people. It's taking away my joy."

Fiona stopped nodding. Joylessness was something she could relate to. Lately she'd been feeling the same way. Maybe it was a good thing she didn't get her stress leave approved. She was going to an exciting new position at the Cosmetic Wellness Centre.

"I want to get up and go to work in a positive and life-affirming atmosphere where people want to better themselves." Dr Wade's stare was fixed like someone undergoing hypnosis.

Positive and life-affirming? That sounded good to her too. Although Fiona didn't understand how cosmetic procedures were life-affirming. To Fiona, life-affirming meant something like volunteering in Africa or working in remote Canada where they needed healthcare workers. But she had to admit, it did sound good. Excited, Fiona's newly resumed head nodding became more animated with the newfound enthusiasm she was feeling.

"Being divorced has made me see my life as a book. I'm now turning the page to a new chapter. But you know the best thing of all, Fiona?"

No, she didn't know what the best thing was. Fiona sat there waiting for him to tell her. It was almost like they were on a friendly basis. "The best thing is that I won't have to see patients who do little to help themselves as I run ragged trying to fix them."

Fiona reflected on what he was saying. (She'd learned to reflect at the 'Putting It All Together' seminar on the last day of Anger Management Three.) Never having been married or divorced, Fiona wondered if this kind of life change happened to everyone when their marriage ended. Then again, he was turning fifty. Fiona knew from experience that turning fifty did weird things to people. *Dear God, now he has no wife, I'm going to have to remember to buy him a birthday cake.*

Continuing to reflect, Fiona knew it wouldn't be easy for some of their patients to find a new doctor. Most doctors had more than enough patients and weren't taking anyone new. Plus, Dr Wade was known to have some of the more challenging clientele. Patients who, for one reason or another, had fired their former doctors. *The receptionist was mean. I had to wait too long. It costs too much to park. She never smiles. My doctor's always late. They're too rushed. He never listens. I need someone closer to where I live.* Not to mention all the ones who expected an instant cure but didn't bother to follow medical advice. All you needed to do was look at Rate Your MD. You did your best for patients, then they went on the site and complained. Made you wonder why they kept coming back if everything was so bad. (Fiona often wished there was a Rate Your Patients website.) But she had to think about herself now. Fiona was going to work at a new place with upbeat and happy people who only wanted to look better. Of course, there had to be a downside, but so far it didn't sound like there was one.

Half-listening to Dr Wade, Fiona started picturing how she

might look with some filler along her laugh lines. Maybe some Botox too. These days a person might feel continually tired, but they didn't have to look that way. She didn't want too much. Fiona had no desire to look like a frozen walleye. She just wanted to knock off five years. Now with the staff discount, she could finally afford it. Hell, maybe she would finally get that pair of boobs she'd been expecting since puberty. Eight years working for Dr Wade and this was the first time she'd felt truly appreciated. Lost in her thoughts, Fiona started warming up to the idea of getting her eyelids done. She was starting to look more like her neighbour's Shar Pei with each passing day. For the first time in a long time, Fiona could say life, and possibly her chins, were looking up.

Picturing her newly-rested-looking face, Fiona noticed Dr Wade was now the one taking deep breaths. He was also gripping the corner of his desk. *Dear God, he's having a heart attack. There goes my non-surgical brow lift.* Dr Wade let go of the desk, stood and came over to her. He looked down at her in what she could only think was a knowing way as he put his hand on her right shoulder. *No! He's taking away my last move.* Was he actually going to apologize for not consulting her before he made such a big decision? And really, what if she hadn't wanted to go? Maybe she liked her job as it was. But Fiona decided to leave well enough alone. She was going to a new office, with new people, in an atmosphere of positivity and beauty. Fiona could always bring his lack of consideration up later. Maybe even use it as leverage for a pay increase.

"Ahem," Dr Wade cleared his throat. He paused as if waiting for her to finally say something.

Like a quick-moving current, Fiona's mind was rushing with

questions. *Maybe I should ask about my training? I'm a nurse after all. Is it too early to ask about the employee discount? There has to be some kind of staff program. A tired and haggard-looking staff member was not good promotion.* But all that could wait. She didn't want to come off as ungrateful for such a wonderful opportunity. Dr Wade brought his watch to his face in a not-so-subtle motion. Fiona decided to ask about the move.

"Dr Wade, when are we planning on moving? I'd like to organize the packing so I know where things are when we get to the new office."

"I'm running late. I was hoping our talk would make things clear."

"Clear?"

"You're not part of the move."

"Dr Wade, it's not a problem. I can pack boxes. I can unpack them too."

"Fiona, I appreciate all you have done over the past eight years. The Wellness Centre doesn't need any more staff. I want to recognize your efforts. I'm giving you one week of pay for every year worked. I've also written you a good reference letter. It's all here." He took a white business envelope from his jacket pocket like a dignitary about to present an official declaration. "I think this is more than fair. Security will escort you to your desk and then out of the office." He leaned down and pressed the help button under his desk.

Brice

For twenty years Brice lived in the West End, the gay hub of Vancouver. His third-floor apartment faced north. Its view of the mountains reminded him of a Group of Seven painting. Of a certain vintage, his building had, for travels up or down, one lone elevator and a flight of stairs. The elevator was as roomy as a hallway closet and always in demand. Most often, whenever the elevator finally did arrive, it opened to an overcapacity crowd with no one budging a nanometer to let anyone else on. Because of this, Brice took to calling the elevator his StairMaster.

Brice hated taking the stairs. His idea of strenuous exercise was to walk from his apartment near Denman Street up the slight incline to the first concession booth in Stanley Park. There he'd have an early dinner. Then, just stuffed, but not overly, from his two pieces of deep-battered fish, greasy chips, coleslaw, and a sugar-glazed cruller, Brice would take the tourist tram around the park. Rides around the park were one of his most favourite things. They brought such lovely sights: blue-turquoise water, lovers holding hands, seagulls circling overhead trying to avail themselves of the daily catch from the paper plates of distracted tourists, and a view of the city all the way to the university endowment lands.

Best of all, no sweating. The only thing that could have made his day any more perfect was if Judy Garland broke out in "The Trolley Song" from *Meet Me in St Louis*. And of course, if Peter were with him.

There were times, however, when taking the stairs wouldn't do. Times when he was laden down with shopping bags, recyclables, or had imbibed one too many wine spritzers after work. But most days, waiting for the elevator wasn't worth the wait. And since he could use the exercise even if he didn't want it, Brice took the stairs. This was especially true on moving days.

After getting home from work one day last spring, Brice had been so tired he decided to wait the interminable wait. He'd spent a long day doing his best with the usual neckties, slippers, and golf clubs for a Father's Day theme. (Everyone said his window with the two dads holding hands looked exceptional.) When the elevator arrived, it was brimming to full with a new tenant's belongings. But his feet hurt, his back ached, and more than anything, he needed Pinot Grigio. So Brice called out a generic welcoming hello to the pink bow barely visible from behind a grey Ikea couch. (Brice never determined someone's pronoun choice until they told him themselves.) Flattening himself between an 80s, floral-print, dusty-rose chair and an ironing board, up they all went. Then somewhere between the second and third floor, the elevator ground to an abrupt stop. The sound it made was like a cartoon locomotive braking on train tracks for a stalled cartoon car. Screaming for oxygen and deliverance, Brice also heaped a large number of curse words on the new occupant for overloading the elevator.

Today, however, coming home after handing in his sick-leave letter, a weariness settled into his bones. As he removed his index finger from the call button, something happened that rarely happened. The doors opened like the parting of the Red Sea and before him lay an empty elevator. This rarity made him think of Mrs Neale. A few weeks before she'd gone into a care facility, someone had left a pile of boxes all over the lobby floor. Brice had been getting his mail when he saw her struggling to get her electric wheelchair around them. After Brice cleared a path, they rode the elevator up together.

"How was your day, Brice?"

"Stressful. I'm dressing the front window for Pride Week. Everyone will be on me like a pack of feral dogs with a ham bone if I don't get it right. Not a detail can be out of place." He remembered looking down at her as she listed to the left, the result of a bad stroke some years prior. "How was your day, Mrs Neale?"

"Better now. Thanks, Brice. I'm so glad for your help. Earlier today, I tried to take the elevator down. It came and went three times before anyone got off to make room for me."

Brice took this as one more sign of the lack of empathy of the masses. Most likely, he believed, a result of the shortfall of compassion education in the Canadian school curriculum. Never would he be able to understand such blatant disregard for someone in need. Now here he was, soon to be the person in need. Would anyone be there to help him? With these thoughts and an empty elevator before him, fighting back his tears, Brice turned and took the stairs.

Brice had no idea who slipped the letter under his door, or when they'd done it. All he knew was that it could be from any of the nutters living in the building: The religious cult on the second floor with a reminder of the Tuesday night save your soul meetings or the Tenant Association with the minutes of the last meeting he hadn't attended, along with a schedule of future meeting dates should he change his mind. It could be another nasty note from his upstairs neighbour demanding Brice turn down his effin' annoying music or else (RuPaul, annoying?). Through an alcohol-induced fog, realizing the volume of his music was unreasonably high due to the wine factor, Brice usually complied with the request. He had no desire whatsoever to learn what "or else" meant.

Neither would Brice have heard a knock. He'd had his head in the fridge, searching for the Pinot Grigio the minute he got through the door. (That empty elevator conjured up deep emotions he couldn't face without fortification.) He wouldn't have heard the knock while he was frying up his quesadilla fixings either—the stove fan was on (and it was better at making noise than at moving air). Then there was his after-dinner cleanup. No way would he have heard a knock then, either. His speakers were cranked to eleven, and he was wearing his favourite apron that read "Nothing Cooks Like Disco" as he danced around his living room to George Michael's "Freedom," a glass of wine in hand.

To Brice, a letter slid under the door was akin to a deed done in the dark by someone wearing night-vision goggles and a balaclava. This feeling was a result of all the letters he'd received over the years from various homophobes informing him he was a freak in need of castrating. So, to prepare for the reading of the letter's contents, Brice topped up his wine, turned off his music, and reclined back to the first notch on his La-Z-Boy. As far as Brice knew, there hadn't been any problems in the building lately. Unless of course the Tenant Association came up with something. There was always something to complain about with that group.

Brice turned over the plain, white envelope labelled "To Mr Brice Sanderson." It must be from Dave, the building manager. He looked haggard lately. Could it be that Dave was finally retiring? He had to be nearing seventy. Although Brice had known him ever since moving into the building twenty years ago and Dave looked seventy then. Brice laughed. Dave probably looked seventy when he was in kindergarten. He took another sip of his wine. Wow, Dave retiring? Maybe now they'd get someone in who could actually fix something. Dave may not have been the best maintenance man but he deserved recognition for his years of service. It was only right. *Dear God. Please no potlucks.*

Brice hated potlucks. They always seemed tawdry and cheap. Not to mention there were always those few that did their share only when it came to eating. A potluck just wasn't good enough for dear old Dave. Brice would see to it that the Tenant Association had the party catered with balloons and dance music, and lots of Dave's favourite, rum. Brice never understood why so many building managers seemed to be heavy drinkers. Until that day he got stuck in the elevator and became one of those hysterical tenants that building managers have to deal with. The building residents just had to do something to give Dave a good send off. After all, he was more of a fixture than the dusty, fake, rubber tree in the lobby.

Opening the letter, Brice looked down at the signature. *When did Dave start using official paper?* Dave was the kind of guy who would give you a message written on a paper towel. Surprise changed to shock, changed to anger, as he read.

To Whom It May Concern:

This is to inform you that improvements will be made to each apartment. All tenants will be given ninety days in which to vacate. Please know you will be given first priority to rent an apartment at fair market pricing.

Yours sincerely,
Dave Turcott, Building Manager

Such devastating news, and the letter wasn't even personalized. Everyone knew there was nothing fair about fair market pricing in Vancouver. This had to be a mistake. Surely this wasn't meant for him? He'd lived here almost as long as anyone in the building had, including Dave. Brice had always paid his rent on time. He was quiet except when overcome by wine and disco. This letter had to be for someone else. Brice looked again at the front of the envelope: "To Mr Brice Sanderson. Apartment #302."

How could this all be happening in one day? He had fucking ALS. He had to stop work because of it. Now some rich-prick-landbarons were telling him he had to move. What was he supposed to do? Go and live with the seagulls in Stanley Park? Brice needed to speak to Dave but he knew better than to call him for elucidation on his eviction notice. Even with the myriad ways of contacting someone these days: a call, a text, an email, a Facebook message, a tweet. Any type of communication during a crisis in the building was a warning bell for Dave to hide. So, draining his glass, Brice got up out of his Lazy-Boy and took the stairs down to suite #101 to talk to Dave the good, old-fashioned way. Mano a mano.

Brice stood before the door of suite #101. He didn't want to be boorish or loud. He decided on three light yet firm raps in quick succession. He was met with silence. Brice knocked again, this time adding more wrist action in case Dave was half-in-the bag or hiding in the bathroom. More silence. His knuckles were red.

"Dave," Brice shouted at the door. "It's Brice. I got the letter. We need to talk."

Nothing. Brice decided it was time for a knock-shout combo. Once again, Brice was met with silence. Was Dave even in there? It was more than likely that Dave had high-tailed it to the nearest bar to avoid the confrontations bound to be coming his way. Brice continued to knock, shout, and repeat.

It is a well-known fact to anyone who has lived in a managed building that managers will do whatever they can to avoid conflict. They dim the lights, turn off the TV, duck behind a wall, pretend they didn't hear you shouting down the hallway. Such times include but are not limited to: when the hot water runs cold, when the cold water runs hot, when the elevator alarm sounds, when a hallway light burns out, when a storage locker is broken into, when the swimming pool has more vegetation in it than the rooftop garden, when the tenant on the fourth floor lets her dog bark all day, and signs of any type of vermin. But a building eviction is a whole other beast. A unifying force, it brings large groups to the manager's door. Soon people from every floor were coming out of the stairwell and the elevator to join Brice. The only person missing was Dave.

"Did you get a letter from Dave?" a voice behind him asked.

"Yes," said a woman wearing a green dress. "Does anyone know what it means?"

"If you came to the Tenant Association meetings or read our minutes, you'd have known this was coming." This from Zola, a middle-aged woman whose thick eyebrows made her look like a 1950s Joan Crawford publicity photo. Zola ran the meetings. Her patronizing attitude was one of the reasons Brice had stopped attending. Plus, she smelled musty. No one else seemed to mind, but musty-smelling people did not agree with him.

"OK," said Green Dress, who, by the tone of her OK had obviously heard this response before. "Now's not the time to go on about people not wanting to attend those boring meetings. All I want to know is why they are asking us to move."

"Well," replied Zola, "this has been happening all over the West End. If you haven't heard of it, and I don't know how you haven't, it's called a renoviction. Owners want to cash in, and developers want to build condos or high-end luxury suites for large profits. They add a splash of paint or change the hallway carpeting, then they jack up the rent. Why would they want us when they can have people with money? It's spread all over Vancouver."

"But I've been a good tenant all these years. I guess I never thought it would happen here," came Green Dress's reply.

"Me too." This from one of the religious nuts on the second floor.

"I've been a good tenant," came a plaintive response. Brice recognized this woman. She was always fundraising in the lobby for her son's school like an offensive linebacker. She'd block tenants from getting to the elevator with what she assumed was a zealous sales pitch that pulled at the heartstrings. Meanwhile, everyone was well aware of little Brian, her son. Brian was the brat caught opening washing machines in full cycle; putting Vaseline on door handles; pressing every button in the elevator, causing the slow elevator trip to go even slower. Now that he was older, this brought with it a new set of problems. The main one being his skateboard. On more than one occasion he'd wheeled into someone in the lobby without a sorry uttered. There was also the noise echoing down the halls. The only person not upset was Mr Fisher, who had the luxury of being able to turn his hearing aid off. Oblivious to their animosity, Brian's mother still kept her fund-raising efforts going. Most people's feelings were that there was little hope for Brian. However, they felt a great deal of empathy for any teacher who had him as a student. And with that in mind, they donated.

"Dave, we know you're in there. You better tell us what this means." This was from the ex-bodybuilder on the second floor. Rumour was he hadn't lifted a weight in ten years. He was so out of shape that even Brice could keep up with him on the stairs. Still, people didn't want to cross him. It was said that he had once practiced some unpronounceable martial art form that could kill with one deadly move. No one wanted to take a chance that he might still be able to render them senseless.

"Ya, Dave. What's 'letter mean?" Miss Dubois slurred, having obviously partaken in one too many scotches.

In what most likely was an attempt to avoid a battered door that might need fixing, Dave opened the door to his apartment just wide enough for him to be partially visible, while still enabling him to make a hasty retreat back into his apartment should there be projectiles. The crowd moved in closer. Brice could understand why Dave hadn't wanted to come out—a small crowd could turn into an angry mob without warning. (One learned this not-so-nice part of human nature when working retail on Christmas Eve. A throng of desperate people could be ruthless.)

"It's just like it says in the letter. They're making improvements to the building," replied Dave.

"How long have you known about this?" Brian-the-Brat's mother asked. "You move us all out, pretending this is a great opportunity. Tell us we can all come back. But we know they'll kick us out and up the rent."

"Yes, you're so right, Linda," said Sandy.

Brice should have known Sandy was on a first-name basis with Brian-the-Brat's mother. When Sandy was a little boy, Brice figured she/they must have been as bratty as Brian. Even now, as a woman, Sandy could be a handful.

"Where are we supposed to go, Dave? Where?"

Brice hadn't seen who said this. The crowd had become too large. It overflowed from the hallway through the lobby, past the mailroom and up into the stairwell. Brice was waiting for someone from the Tenant Association to start telling them they were breaking some kind of fire safety rule.

"They tell me the same thing they tell you!" barked Dave. "I know they won't need a building supervisor. They're a management company for cryin' out loud. They'll have concierges in uniforms. I'll be out too!"

Suddenly it was all becoming too real. Brice looked around at the crowd that had gathered. He knew many of them. Over the years, you got to talking when you met in the mail room. Or when pressing the code to open the front entrance, or while waiting in the lobby for a cab when the weather was bad. Some he'd known from the bar scene he used to hang out in with Peter. Now they were all being forced out, his community gone.

"My ass, we've got to vacate. They just want to raise the rent, is all they want. We're going to fight this thing," said the ex-bodybuilder.

As a few heads nodded in agreement, Zola, her eyebrows meeting together like two caterpillars kissing, looked around in frustration. "I know what you all think of me and the Tenant Association. I often wonder why I bother. Until things affect you personally, no one cares. But now we're at the crunch, you all want to take up the banner like you're the first in line. Let me tell you, in case you didn't know, fighting this will give us six months, tops. Every other case like this has been lost. A few of the renters in the early court cases got more time before they eventually got evicted, but it's been going on for years now. Building owners are so used to doing this, they know how to deal with the courts. By the time we pay lawyers and court costs when we lose, and we will lose, it just isn't worth it financially or emotionally. You'd know all this if you came to meetings."

Brice rolled his eyes upward like he was searching for something on the ceiling. If there was an earthquake followed by a tsunami followed by a mudslide, that woman could turn it into a rant about the Tenant Association. *God, I might even miss the Tenant Association.* Brice looked around as the crowd started to disperse. A few mentioned going for drinks. A couple asked when the next Tenant Association meeting was. Miss Dubois was crying and being comforted by Sandy. Even bratty Brian was trying to console her. Brice just wanted to go back to his wine and disco.

Already three people deep, there was no hope of taking the elevator. Climbing up the stairs to his apartment, Brice looked for the long-standing dust ball on the landing area between the first and second floors. Besides being a bad maintenance man, Dave wasn't all that good with a broom. The dust ball was still there. Somehow for Brice, in this world where everything was so easily gotten rid of, that dust ball had become a symbol of permanence. *Maybe I should take it with me? God, how much wine have I had?* Was it really only six months ago that he'd wanted to give everything up, retire early, and travel the world? Now all he wanted was his health, his job, and his apartment back. With ALS and ultimately needing more care, Brice knew he'd eventually have to move. It was just that he wanted to make his own decision on when that move would happen. Now even that was being taken away from him.

Brice headed over to his coffee table. He needed music. Within easy reach, his favourite playlist—a 70s remix—was waiting. For Brice, music was the sound of the soul being made real. As he waited for the opening notes, he wiped away the tears with the back of his hand. *Why me? What did I do to deserve all this badness?* And then, from his portable speaker, the sounds of an angel played out just for him. "I Will Survive" by the great disco diva Gloria Gaynor. Brice started dancing. While he still could.

Adelina

Like a scavenger bird on a carcass, all week Adelina's conversation with Dr Lovell ate away at her. She hated this feeling of complicity. Joni was her friend. Adelina owed it to her to tell her what was happening with their jobs. For sure, Joni would tell her if she was the one who found out first.

She tried talking to Don about the changes at work but he just stared off into the distance. His blank look let her know the monster was out. That the game had begun. Anything from being talked down to or to being hit. Adelina never knew which was coming. Sometimes the monster gave her a head start. Let her know what she'd done wrong. Those times she felt like an escapee running on wet rocks, trying to escape the hounds. Other times, when Don didn't tell her what she'd done, Adelina felt like she was in a guessing game with no one sending her clues. Either way, she knew how it ended. How it always ended. Their one-bedroom apartment afforded no hiding places. And now work, her sanctuary, was in jeopardy. Even prayer did not give directions to an escape route. It was as if God was saying, "I told you so."

She'd seen signs of the monster's existence before they married. A sideways glimpse of a cringing face, a tortured grimace, anger in the eyes. All suggesting something. All disappearing when Adelina turned to get a better look. And that was what made the monster so devious. It lay in wait until after their marriage to fully introduce itself. Almost unnoticed, it crept its way into her life, isolating her from family and friends—all those who may have helped her.

Adelina had tried to ask for help. Tried to ask for advice. Tried to talk about the violence. Once. After their engagement. She told her mother there was a side to Don she wasn't sure about.

"Adelina, it will be good. God is giving you a husband to take care of you. You can have a family. Have a home of your own." Adelina could see her parents were just happy someone was taking her away. It meant they'd have one less mouth to feed and maybe the promise of help. Money, labour—a dowry of sorts from their daughter's new husband. After that one time, Adelina never brought the monster's violence up to anyone. If her own family wouldn't listen, why would anyone else?

Today, coming home from work, it didn't take long to find out what the crazy maker was. "I was looking forward to having some peanut butter on my toast. Now I can't." Soon he'd be telling her how little there was in his life—such a small effort for him to be happy, and here she was ruining everything.

Adelina went to the pantry. It was really only a broom closet but Adelina liked the word. Pantry. Food from a pantry sounded homemade and cared for and special. Let me go to the pantry and get you something. That's what they said in those old cowboy movies she loved. In those movies, an actress could make a jar of peaches sound wholesome and good, like the best thing you could ever eat. Adelina loved to watch as the poor widow, whose husband had died from the flu, was left to tend the farm. All the farm hands were gone because the widow couldn't pay them. But there was always that one man who came riding up on his horse, hiding out from his demons or the law, maybe both, who helped her work the land. Of course, she couldn't pay him until the crops came in. But he had a place to stay and he always got a share of her meagre provisions. Sometimes they killed a chicken that had stopped laying. There was always something for them to deal with as they saved the farm from drought and pestilence and invaders. By the end of the movie, they were in love, married, got to keep the farm, and gosh-darn if she wasn't pregnant.

Children. Adelina had so wanted children, but when she didn't get pregnant after twelve years of marriage, of course like everything else, it was her fault. Nothing to do with Don and his lack of desire for anything but the drink. So, she gave up on that dream too.

In Adelina's pantry, there was rarely anything special. Today there was no peanut butter. There wouldn't be any either, until the end of the week when she got her pay. Why, she thought, coming out of the pantry empty-handed, was it her fault there was none left? Why was it always the case that when things ran out, or stopped working, or cost too much it was because of her? But Adelina knew the answer. To the monster, everything that was wrong was because of her. To the monster, Adelina was what was wrong. Now, closing the pantry curtain, she knew the monster would be waiting for his peanut butter and his answers. Adelina had neither. She felt like asking Don what he did around the house besides eating and drinking and sleeping. But asking such questions was backtalk. And backtalk meant one thing from Don when he was the monster. Pain. Adelina had learned many things during her married life besides the fact that monsters don't like back-talk. Monsters don't let you leave.

Getting ready for work that night, Adelina took out the button-up work shirt with the long sleeves. The monster did his hurting where it wouldn't show. Joni had guessed long ago why Adelina sometimes wore long sleeves to work. But that night at work, Joni didn't say anything. Truth was, Joni had barely said anything all week. Adelina knew it was the hole coming between them. The hole she created by not telling Joni the truth. There was such deep sorrow in Adelina's heart. Not only for the chasm between her and Joni but also for the changes coming to everyone's jobs, unsettling all their lives.

Adelina prayed to God for guidance. If she stayed at her job there would be twice the work. Sooner or later, they'd cut wages. Companies always did. Anything to make their shareholders happy. Adelina so wanted to tell Joni about what was coming. Ask her friend what they should do—stay or go? But she had also promised Dr Lovell not to say anything. Adelina was good at that. But not, she would soon learn, as good as Joni.

Starting her shift that night, Adelina joined in the ritual. The staff met in the supply room, packing their mops, brooms, and cleaning supplies. This was the time everyone would catch up with each other. They'd listen to complaints about poor sleep. How someone else's cruise of a lifetime went. Or how another's divorce was going. A few had daycare issues affecting their work schedules. Then, carts ready, off they'd all roll to the elevators to get to their assigned floors. There'd be no more time for chats during the work night. Each team intentionally scheduled a different break time on their different floors. In the morning, with their work done, there might be a few minutes to talk. Mostly there was only enough energy left to clean up and go home to bed.

"This is the employer's strategy to separate and divide us," Joni had told Adelina when they were first getting to know each other. "They don't want us congregating and forming a union." But the worst thing about not congregating was that it kept great ideas from forming. And even though Joni didn't like most of the people they worked with and didn't want to talk to them if she could help it, she'd say to Adelina, "We need to band together. There's strength in numbers." Adelina was so proud of Joni when she heard her talk like that. It gave her hope. Made her see things in a different way. When Joni talked like that Adelina could almost see a brighter future for herself.

That night, as everyone gathered in the storeroom to get ready for work, the talking started. What food someone had made for their break, what someone else was planning for their upcoming holiday, how a visit to a sick parent went. There was the usual banter about getting a poker game going. This was just talk, though. There wasn't enough time to get a game started, never mind finish it. Besides, everyone knew hell would be raised if pay cheques were lost. They were already small enough.

As they rolled their carts toward the elevator, Pete, their supervisor who usually stayed back, called out for them to listen up. This rarely happened. To stop meant no work was being done and, to Office Cleaning Supply, time was money.

"A mandatory meeting has been called by the company. Each and every one of you needs to come back half an hour earlier in the morning. All of you." He said this looking around to make sure everyone heard him. The only other time Adelina could remember a mandatory meeting was after a couple of cleaners had tried to start a union. They and their plans for a union vote were gone the next morning. Everyone got the message—unions, fair wages, and good benefits were not allowed at this job.

After Pete left, the rumblings started: It must be about the contract. They must have gotten it renewed. What if they didn't? Whatever it is, it can't be good. Adelina kept silent, her head down. They'd all learn what was happening soon enough. And there was her promise. One thing was for sure, Adelina never wanted to keep such a secret ever again. Holding knowledge about people's lives was a heavy burden.

On the way to the elevator, Jackie said she'd heard there was some kind of job shuffling happening. A few murmured in agreement.

"Who the fuck wants our jobs?" asked Frank, Jackie's job partner. This was met with nervous laughs.

Adelina didn't like such language, even at times like this. But she could understand why he used it. He'd been working graveyard for three years now, Jackie for fifteen. They all knew this was a dead-end job. Yet they all needed it. There were few places for any of them to go. The company knew this too. Misfortune had guided them along this path.

"Stop with the jokes, Frank. Just be here in the morning," Pete warned, sneaking up from behind.

At the elevator door, Adelina waited for Joni to say something. Adelina could tell everyone else was waiting too. But Joni just looked down at her phone. Gossip was that Joni and Pete were involved, but Adelina knew better. Joni was always saying that getting involved with management never ended well. If things went sideways, the worker was the one who got the axe. Besides, Adelina knew Joni would tell her if she was involved with Pete. She and Joni were work partners but they were also friends.

As they rode up the elevator, the silence was a fissure between them. *I'm going to tell her.* How could Adelina have kept such news to herself and not shared it with her best friend? But as they both headed to the first office, Joni said: "I'd like to work on my own tonight. I have to think."

Adelina, silent, nodded. She so badly wanted to ask what was wrong, but the secret Adelina was holding felt like a deep hole she couldn't climb out of. Adelina only hoped all the rumours about their work contract didn't make Joni return to the bottle.

That shift was one of the longest and loneliest nights of Adelina's life. Joni not only wanted to work alone, she also took her break on her own. Now it was time for the meeting. Adelina waited for Joni to gather up her supplies before heading down, but Joni told her to go ahead. There was something she needed to finish up first. Adelina still so desperately wanted to say something, but it was too late. *God,* Adelina prayed silently as she waited for the elevator, *please let Joni understand. I made that promise to Dr Lovell. I couldn't break it.*

Back in the supply room, Adelina took a look around. Everyone looked exhausted and drained. This was nothing new. What was new was the fear on their faces.

"Where is that soul mate of yours?" Joe asked. "It's not like her to be late getting off work."

"She's coming in a minute," Adelina answered.

"Maybe I should've been late too," Lori, his workmate, joked.

"For sure this won't be good news. It's always the first fired is the last hired."

"I think you've got that reversed, Lori," said Joe.

"Same thing in the end."

"Says the English lit major," answered Joe.

"Won't be if I lose my job. School doesn't pay for itself." Lori looked down at her cart.

"It will be OK, Lori," Joe said, gently touching her shoulder.

Some of the other workers nodded in sympathy, but most, Adelina knew, were doing the numbers in their heads, trying to remember who had recently talked of retiring or quitting and who had less seniority. All things that might make their own jobs safe.

"Face it," said Frank behind his cart. "Every last one of us needs this job. We work hard. We show up night after night. We don't get to see much of our loved ones. We clean dirt and shit and piss for just above minimum wage. Each and every one of us takes pride in this fucking job. All so we can clean more filth. They should be offering us a raise, not scaring us with a veiled threat."

When all of the cleaners were finished, they were met not only by Pete but another man. This other man, dressed in his expensive suit, looked like a model in a men's magazine. On the table in front of them was a large stack of manila folders. Each tab lined-up facing outward, a tower of bad news. To the right was another stack of papers equally as high. Adelina had no idea what to make of this. Neither could she decipher the look on either of their faces. If Joni were beside her, Adelina knew she would say they were wearing poker faces. Joni always said you needed one of those when you were dropping the axe.

Behind her someone snickered. "At least head office knows how it feels to be up this early in the morning." No one turned to see who had spoken. They didn't want to give him away. More importantly, they didn't want to be seen agreeing with him.

The man in the suit started to speak. "For those who don't know, I am Mr Kenneth Fraser, from head office. I want to thank you all for getting your work done and coming back early. I'll try and keep this meeting short. I know you all need to get home."

The voice in Adelina's head sounded like Joni. When someone dressed in a suit comes in early to work to tell you something, you know it can only be bad news. *Where was Joni?* Adelina kept her face forward. She could not afford to look uninterested.

Mr Kenneth Fraser continued talking in an official-sounding voice. "We've been in negotiations with the building owners. The contract, as you know, is up. They were considering not renewing." Adelina felt her breath stop. "Luckily, we have been able to renegotiate the contract." Adelina felt her shoulders drop. She let out the breath she was holding. Something must have changed since her talk with Dr Lovell. "Unfortunately, there will be job losses," added Mr Kenneth Fraser.

A loud moan came from the group. Lori was crying. This wasn't only about lost jobs and not being able to provide for their families. That was a weighty enough chain to drag along. It was about their dreams. Dreams of finally owning a car, paying for tuition, taking a trip back to their home country, saving for a down payment on something small and almost affordable outside the city limits. Dreams were the fuel that kept them going. They left these dreams unspoken for fear that, if they said them out loud, they would drift away into non-existence. Now with this news, their futures were evaporating before them.

"Will one of them be your stinking job?" yelled Tony, who grew up in the days when grade ten could get you into a good-paying job. He had one too, until the paper mill closed. Cleaning was all he could get now.

Mr Kenneth Fraser looked at Pete. "We're just doing our jobs. Management is also cutting positions. There have already been cuts at head office."

"What the fuck do you do there, anyway," shouted Frank. Adelina heard from Joni that Frank had gambling debt. He'd been fired from his good-paying office job for stealing from the social fund. Only low-paying, unskilled cleaning jobs like this gave folks a second chance. If chance was even the right word.

Behind Frank, nodding her head, was Mary, who'd once been a teacher. Rumour was she made a misbehaving kid go outside in winter without a coat. That had not been the first time. The teachers' union was strong, but even they couldn't save her license. Adelina tried to tell her about God, but Mary told Adelina she had wine to save her. She didn't need anything else.

Looking around the room, Adelina knew that many of her co-workers' lives were not as they had planned. They'd lost good-paying jobs due to downsizing or closing up shop or some transgression on their part. Adelina had had her own bumpy road—leaving school after grade twelve and getting married at twenty. Don too, getting injured at work and having to go on disability, then failing his retraining. She and Don were both free-falling, tumbling head over heels. But sometimes, in her despair, Adelina saw the hard ground as a welcome mat.

Mr Kenneth Fraser was speaking again. Adelina knew he was

delaying the bad news with his fancy speech. In her head, Adelina could hear Joni. "They fill you full of crap about how great a job you have been doing before they bring out the knife and stab you."

"We want to thank all of you for your efforts," Mr Kenneth Fraser said. "We know some of you have been journeying along with us since the inception of the company. It has been twenty years. Office Cleaning Services could not have done it without you. I won't lie: negotiating this contract has been difficult. We had to make some drastic concessions. We have your lay-off notices ready. If you want to apply for a position, we also have applications." The axe had come down.

"What do you mean, 'lay-off notices'?" Frank demanded. Adelina thought Frank should be quiet. Didn't he know by now that nothing he said would make any difference? Nothing anyone said would make a difference.

Mr Kenneth Fraser continued. "We are handing out lay-off notices. You can apply for a position. Just be aware that, going forward, there will be two-thirds of the positions available. There will also be reductions in pay."

"What kind of fucking negotiations are these?" Frank yelled. "Where the fuck did you go to school? Any idiot who thinks more work for less pay is a success is stupider than I am."

"Remember, no need to get foul." This came from Pete.

"What if we don't come in to work tonight?" asked Frank, desperately looking around at the crowd, hoping to gather support.

"Well Frank," said Pete, "that won't look good on your resume now, will it?"

"The short hairs," Tony whispered to Adelina. "That's what they've got us by."

Not only would there be changes to their work, but they would also have to compete with each other for their jobs? This could get messy quickly. Adelina pulled at her sleeves. Where was Joni?

Mr Kenneth Fraser was speaking again. "Pete has been moved to the site across the street. I want to thank him for his ten years of service here at the Medical Centre Building. Now, let me introduce your new on-site supervisor. Please, everyone, a big round of applause for Ms Joni Howard."

Joni? Joni was going to be the new supervisor? This couldn't be right. This couldn't be right at all. They were friends. They worked together every night, yet Joni hadn't said a thing. That had to mean Joni knew about the contract and the layoffs. All this time, when she herself had been keeping Dr Lovell's secret, Joni had been keeping an even bigger one. Only now, the secret was out. Joni was going to be their supervisor, while the rest of them had to re-apply to get their jobs back. If they could get their jobs back.

Joni came forward from the back of the room. "It was after much consideration that I accepted the position of building supervisor. I feel safe in the knowledge that, together, the successful applicants and I can move forward with the new contract." Adelina could no longer look at Joni. Joni was sounding like the kind of person she usually made fun of. Now she was one of them. Joni continued: "Please, everyone, this is a difficult time. I know you need to get home. Your lay-off notices are up here at the front. You all have two months before this contract ends. When you receive your notice, if you're interested, you're welcome to pick up a job application. I'll start by calling your names."

"That's it?" Frank called out. "That's fucking it? We can apply for our jobs? Some of us have families. We all have bills. We need to eat. All of us have worked hard for this company. Why do we need to reapply for our own jobs? What did you know, Joni? You were one of us until this morning. I bet there's fucking foreign workers waiting down the hall, ready to take our jobs from us. You're so full of crap with your uppity ways, Joni Howard. You know many of us don't stand a chance of keeping our jobs."

Silence answered Frank. Adelina knew he was right. Why had Dr Lovell even bothered to take her aside that morning? She and everyone in that room were all just pieces on a chessboard and they were being played. For just one day, Adelina would like to be the queen controlling the board.

Ignoring Frank, Joni started calling out names. It felt as if they were waiting for the executioner. Finally, her name was called, and Adelina crossed the room. *They're all looking at me.* Adelina hadn't noticed such attention paid to the others who had already been to the front. Some were blatantly staring. *God, please give me the strength to hold my own.*

Joni looked Adelina straight in the eye. "Here's your lay-off notice, Adelina." Joni handed her an envelope. "Let me get you a job application," Joni said, handing her a form from the dwindling stack before her. No one else had been handed one.

"No thank you, Ms Howard. I need to work for a company I can trust." Adelina turned and walked out.

At the bus stop, Adelina looked up at the sky. It was strange to find no one from work waiting with her. No loyalty left, except to themselves and their families; the starving rats were probably making their pitch for that last piece of cheese—their jobs. If Adelina were to add this morning up—losing her job, two mouths to feed, most likely the end of her friendship with Joni—none of it equalled hope. Yet, somehow, she felt more whole than she'd felt for a very long time. Maybe this was her fresh start? The new beginning she'd been waiting for most of her life.

The bus lurched to a stop before her. Tired, she climbed up the steps, a hiker on the last leg before the summit. On the bus, the morning work crowd was packed in tight, all freshly washed and ready for the day ahead. Adelina looked down the aisle. People were staring at their phones. Others were listing back and forth as they slept their way to work. A few wore headphones shouting out music. No one made a move to give their seat to the old, pregnant, or disabled. Kindness and good manners had become a lost language. A feeling of darkness passed over her as she realized the hope she'd felt only a few minutes before was gone. Adelina had dropped it on the street as she climbed onto the bus. Now her thoughts turned to home. What would the monster say?

Spring/Summer 2019

Fiona

Maybe I should work in retail? Fiona looked down at the Waterview Retirement Village ad on her bathroom counter. She needed a job, but was this really the one? Working in an old folk home? On the night shift? At her age, seven years to official retirement?

She read the inspirational post-it note taped to her mirror—"Your Thoughts Become Your Actions." Her beauty skin routine complete, she needed some make-up. But not too much. Fiona didn't want to look like she was interviewing for clown school. She peered into the mirror and moved her head left and right, up and down. The part on the top of her head was starting to look like a river on a topographic map. (No one told you about ageing and female pattern hair loss.) Fiona tossed her hair with her hands. It might be thinning, but at least her curls helped hide her scalp from shining through. She smiled into the mirror and then relaxed her face. Her crow's feet used to only show when she was smiling. Now they were permanent fixtures. It seemed to Fiona that every part of her body was heading south. She picked up the Waterview ad from the counter.

After a good breakfast (past experience warned that a growling stomach did not go well at an interview), Fiona headed to her bedroom to get dressed. The last time she'd worn her one casual business suit, it was for her job interview with Dr Wade. That was eight years and twenty pounds ago.

Dressed, Fiona assessed her efforts before her full-length mirror. Even with Spanx reigning things in, her bulging stomach pulled the skirt taut. The button at the breast of her crisp white shirt looked loose. She took a deep breath to check on its status. If it was going to pop, it'd better pop now and not during her interview. Finally, one good yank of her pantyhose and they were as high up at the crossroads as they could go. As far as Fiona could tell, she oozed professionalism. She picked up her purse with her neatly folded, slightly embellished resume and the Waterview ad inside it. Sensible shoes on, Fiona grabbed her raincoat and locked the door.

Another boastful selling point for Waterview Retirement Village was its close proximity to transit. Fiona took a look at her fellow travellers. The line-up of people folding in on itself told her this wouldn't be the happy commuting experience suggested in their ad. *Please God, don't let the drunk guy talking to himself sit beside me. Or the man with the dirty bandages falling off his legs, also talking to himself. Or the two ladies shouting at each other. Don't need them either.* Fiona walked to the end of the lineup.

Later than the schedule promised, the standing-room-only #20 bus crawled its way up the incline to the stop. Fiona climbed on, then slowly made her way down the gauntlet to the back of the bus. Nobody was going to miss this bus because she didn't move to the back to make room, unlike others, who took a spot and just stood there like cement statues, not budging an inch to make room. Not able to move back any farther, Fiona grabbed onto the dangling overhead strap. This circus balancing act was one of the many reasons she hated taking public transit. The man beside her shouting into his phone was another.

She moved her face into an opening between a man's armpit and the top of an older, bent woman's sombrero. There was just enough space to see out the bus's glass door. Alongside, a car was waiting for the light to change. The driver was laughing as the passenger pressed something on her phone. *They're probably listening to music they like. Not like the stuff screaming out of that guy's headphones.* Fiona looked over at the young man standing beside her, oblivious to the correlation between high volume levels and hearing loss. *Bet those two are in temperature-controlled comfort. Nothing like the sweaty mess of humanity I'm standing in—no one's coughing or hacking all over those two. Carbon footprint or no carbon footprint, everyone on this tin can would jump at the chance to hitch a ride.* Another passenger searching for a place to stand inched their way into Fiona's line of vision. It seemed to Fiona that car travel was the last bastion of comfort and self-agency left in the free world.

Without warning, the bus jerked to an abrupt stop. An angry voice called out Fiona's thoughts: "What the Hell?" Another voice aimed slurs at the driver. Someone else jolted awake, his voice sounding panicked as he shouted, "Is this my stop?" Crowded-in like third-class passengers on the Titanic, for all Fiona knew, they could have hit an iceberg.

"Sorry for that, folks. A cyclist in the lane doesn't want to share the road. You know, the kid in the sandbox situation," announced the bus driver overhead.

"Stinking cyclists" cried another woman unseen by Fiona. "There's a bike lane one block over. Can't they use that for fuck's sake?"

This bus ride was doing nothing to help her maintain Fiona's positive attitude. She squeezed her face into the opening left after the sombrero got off the bus. She looked to see if anyone was making a move to get out of their seat. Instead, Fiona saw a young woman sitting in the single row below her, applying mascara in front of a small travel mirror. She had to be fighting some kind of law. But what? Gravity? Nature? Good manners? It amazed Fiona that with all the jerking and stopping the woman hadn't poked her eye out. Fascinated, Fiona continued to watch as the woman packed up her mascara and put it in her purse. Then, taking out her blusher and brush like an artist before an easel, started applying colour to her cheeks. Beside Fiona, the man was still shouting into his phone.

Finally, the computer-generated voice garbled something that sounded like the name of her stop. As the bus braked, the owner of the armpit swayed, almost falling on top of her. Heading to the door to get off, another passenger stepped hard on Fiona's left foot. Then apologizing repeatedly, promptly stepped on her right. Fiona felt like a wilted flower needing rain. She only hoped her professional business look still appeared professionally business-like by the time she got to her interview. Grateful to be set free, Fiona made her way to the exit and got off the bus.

She held her hand upward. Vancouver's spring rains seemed to start the minute you stepped outside. She pulled her hood over her hair. Then, taking cover under the awning of a closed business, Fiona looked at her hard copy map of the Waterview Retirement

Village. Azealia and Begonia Towers sat side by side in the front. Further back, out of sight, sat Calla Lily Tower with its own parking lot. Her interview would be held there. The theme of the place wasn't lost on her. Waterview Retirement Village was misappropriating the tranquillity of exotic flowers to name their buildings. In simpler times, these buildings would be known as A, B, and C, respectively. No matter what the names, Fiona knew the ascent up the alphabet corresponded to the progressive decline of the inhabitants. Such configurations were intended to keep the healthy-aged from the infirm-aged. Should her interview be successful, Calla Lily Tower would be where Fiona would work. She looked down at her watch. Perfect. Even with the bus being late, she was on time for her interview.

Without a word, the young man asked to show Fiona to the interview room and took his cell phone from his back pocket. Not a step missed, head bent in the ubiquitous prayer-like vigil to the cell phone god, he started texting. *Just when did "text" become a verb?* Fiona watched his step lighten as he bounced ahead of her. Stopping mid-way down the hall, he opened a door on the left and pointed to a chair. "Have a seat." Fiona heard the door close behind her as she sat down.

Surreptitiously, Fiona took a look around. (You never knew if there were cameras.) The walls were grey. What was it with grey? Blue-grey. Black-grey. Just grey. It was as if there were no other colours left in the world to paint walls with. Occasionally, someone painted a purple or green feature wall. Still, it was all so depressing. Next year it was her turn for the management company to paint her apartment. No way was she letting them paint it grey again. She wanted pimento.

Fiona looked to the left at the chair, sister to the one she was sitting in. They looked to be from one of those big office supply places. Somewhere, she had read that the purchase of office furniture was related to organizational spending habits. For example, if an employer skimped on your chair, what else were they willing to forgo to save money? Fiona felt along the underside of her chair. *Ah, levers.* That same article said that chairs with levers showed a direct correlation between how much an employer cared about their employees and how much they didn't. It had to do with ergonomics. No levers, no caring. Fiona removed her hand. It wouldn't make a good impression if she were found jack-knifed.

Pay attention. Exude a positive, confident, capable aura. Fiona sat up straight, her feet planted firmly, following the YouTube video's advice. Her eyes focused on the rectangular, oak desk before her. Few bought oak anymore. It was too heavy in weight and in look. Here, it was out of place with the grey walls and the black accessorizing of the other furniture. Either a resident tried moving it into their suite, then found it took up too much space and gave it to Waterview, or they died lifting it. Fiona laughed to herself. It could also be due to a culture of organizational thrift. Waterview may have purchased it cheap from a second-hand furniture shop. With her own British-Canadian protestant background, she leaned toward the utilitarian, lasts-a-lifetime look of the hand-me-down. The cherrywood sideboard taking up too much space in her one-bedroom apartment attested to this.

It seemed to Fiona, for some unknown reason, that offices these days go with more of a Scandinavian design. The cold, sparse look of the Nordic peoples' furniture was something Fiona couldn't understand. Plus, you had to put things together yourself after you paid good money for them. After two weeks assembling her bed, then finding herself with an extra screw, even now, three years later, Fiona kept waiting for the bed to crash in on her. Why did today's consumers not see they were doing all the work? They checked out their own purchases at the grocery store. They banked online. They searched airline websites to find out what country their luggage ended up in. To Fiona's mind, consumers were being tricked into work that should have been done by a company's employees. Those companies that still had employees. *Speaking of employees.* She glanced down at her watch. Twelve minutes late.

Fiona looked across the desk. To the left stood a lamp with a grey shade (no surprise there). To the right stood a green fig tree. Without touching it, Fiona couldn't tell if the plant was real or not. On the wall directly in front of her hung a print of a typical Canadian landscape, trees around a body of water. The Great Lakes? Hudson Bay? One of the 1,000 lakes in Manitoba? Fiona looked around the room again. This office was so nondescript it could be anywhere in Canada.

If something was described as nondescript, wasn't it, in fact, being described? So really, that meant there was no such thing as nondescript. Fiona lifted her hand to her hair. Then, not wanting to be caught fixing herself up should the interviewer appear, placed her hand back in her lap. *I probably look like a chia pet. I hope my eyeliner isn't smudged. If I wait much longer, I'll need to pee. Not even offered a glass of water. I'm on time. Why isn't my interviewer?*

She looked down at her watch again. Twenty minutes late without a word. Was this one of those power plays they warned about on YouTube? Not that she could remember what YouTube said to do in a power play.

Finally, a knock interrupted her thoughts. A woman at least twenty-five years her junior came toward her, hand outstretched. As she shook it, Fiona did the math. When this girl was born, Fiona was listening to a Sony CD Walkman. Fiona shook the hand offered.

"Hello, my name is Christine Terry. So nice to meet you." Nothing mentioned about being late and leaving Fiona to sit there like a big, old, lonely turd. That was the thing Fiona admired about the younger generations; they were good at deflecting any negativity you might try and throw at them before you got a chance to throw it.

"So nice to meet you, at last, Ms Terry. Call me Fiona."

"We're a little late so I think we should get started."

We? Twenty minutes without warning was not, in Fiona's estimation, a little. What it was was rude.

"Yes. I'm sure you're busy." *Unlike me. I can sit here all day waiting because I have nothing else to do.*

"Do you have any questions before we get started, Fiona?"

"Are you the only one sitting in on the interview?" Fiona asked.

"Yes."

Like the sun shining after a monsoon, a wave of relief washed over Fiona. She smiled happily at Christine. Fiona had heard more than one worrying tale about panel interviews.

"Let me qualify that. For our first interview," Christine said.

The first interview? Dear God, not another job where they have you coming back over and over again like you're interviewing to replace the prime minister of Canada.

"So today we'll have our interview. Then, if you meet the criteria for the position, the director of operations will meet with you along with one of the other registered nurses."

What happened to just handing in your resume, getting an interview, waiting to hear back, then getting the yeah or nay? "Thanks, Christine, for clarifying. I look forward to meeting them." Fiona hoped her smile looked genuine.

"OK, why don't we start."

To prepare for her interview, Fiona had watched two YouTube videos. The first: "Five Top Interview Techniques with Donna." The second: "How to Nail Your Interview and Get the Job." With no recent interview experience of her own and with most of her friends not having any recent interview experience from which to draw (her friends, ensconced in their careers for years, were all hoping to add to their pensionable service by hanging onto their jobs by the skin of their teeth), Fiona had nowhere else to turn.

"If you were an animal, which one would you be and why?" Donna had asked, looking into the camera. Fiona assumed Donna's pause meant she was actually waiting for an answer.

"I would be a dog, Donna. A dog is loving and loyal and watches over you," Fiona answered, looking back at the screen. Sloth, Fiona knew, was not a good answer.

James, the young man on "How to Nail Your Interview and Get the Job," was more direct. "What are you? A hunter or a gatherer?" This seemed like a trick question. It wasn't as if she was applying to be Zog's replacement after a T-Rex sat on him. What did such a question have to do with anything anyway? This is what came with human resources being privatized. All of them hanging onto their own jobs by coming up with idiotic interview questions.

Christine picked up her pen and put it on the pad on the oak desk. "Fiona, if I were to ask if you are a hunter or a gatherer, which would you be?"

Really, Christine. You're asking that one? "A gatherer. I like to look for solutions and bring them back," Fiona answered, smiling sweetly. Hunting things down and killing them did not sound like good nursing qualities.

"Thank you." Christine smiled, looking up after scratching something on her notepad. "Can you tell me what your strength is?"

Going for lunch? "My honesty." Fiona smiled again.

Christine's head moved up and down like an old-time Dachshund bobblehead on a rear dash. Christine's head stopped bobbing. She looked at Fiona, her pen mid-air, a conductor pausing, preparing the orchestra to play. "Why is that?"

"Well," Fiona looked over Christine's head at the lake. *It would be so nice to go for a swim.* "I believe if we are honest, in a thoughtful and respectful manner, we can all get along. This helps make for an environment everyone can enjoy." *Please let that be good enough.* Christine scratched something else on her pad.

"Can you name a time you had to deal with conflict in the workplace?" Christine laid down her pen again and looked at Fiona.

When wasn't there conflict? "Well, I remember staying late once, after a very hectic day at work. My former employer told me to go home, but, Christine, I just couldn't. There was simply too much work left to complete. I wanted to finish it so it wouldn't impact the workload for the next day. So I stayed," Fiona brown-nosed. For good measure, she beamed a saintly smile. *So much for being honest.*

"Anything else you would like to add?" Christine looked at her watch as she picked up her pen.

"Yes, Christine. I know you will find me to be hard-working and patient-focused. I am open to new ideas. I believe I am the candidate for this job." Fiona looked directly at Christine. Both Donna and James would be proud of her.

"Thank you for that, Fiona. If you are a successful candidate, we will be in touch. We will give you a tour of the facility then. Are you able to follow the red line out to the entrance? Or would you like someone to accompany you?"

"Not a problem, Christine. I look forward to hearing from you." With that Fiona followed the red line to the entrance, still not certain if she did or didn't want the job.

Like a matador before the bull, Fiona steeled herself. She hadn't called home in weeks. "Hi, Mom. How are you?" Fiona hoped the added inflection at the end of the sentence made her sound upbeat.

"I'm good, dear. But if you'd call more often, you'd know that. What's wrong?" Fiona could hear the concern in her mother's voice. She could picture her at the other end of the line, sitting upright, leaning into her landline.

"What do you mean by wrong?" *Fifty-eight and still defending myself.*

"Fiona, when I don't hear from you in a while, I know something's up." Her mother was like one of those dogs that sensed bad weather before it came.

"Mom. That's not true." The space between her and her mother was filled with half-truths. "I'm calling to see how you're doing. I realize I haven't called lately. It's just that, with the time change, by the time I remember to call, it's too late. I figure you're probably in bed." For the most part, this was true. Other times it was because Fiona didn't have the emotional energy. The mountain that was her mother's expectations was a high climb. As for Fiona's father, he died seven years ago.

"You could get up earlier and call me before work, you know. There's always weekends too. You might try calling then."

"Well, Mom, I do have news. I've changed jobs." Fiona braced herself for her mother's book-cover version of her work life.

"Another new job? I thought you said you were happy with that doctor's office. Fiona, if there's a revolving door for jobs, you seem to be stuck in it. What happened this time?"

"Well, Mom, Dr Wade decided to close the practice. No one else was willing to take it over." Fiona decided to skip the Wellness Centre part of the closure. No need for her mother to know Fiona hadn't made the cut.

"Closing his practice? I didn't realize he was old enough to retire. He looked younger than that when I was out to visit three years ago. Is he sick? You can't stay with the doctor taking over?"

"Dr Wade isn't old or sick. I guess with half the runway of his life gone, he wants to make a change. These days a doctor could put up a cardboard sign on a street corner announcing they were opening an office under the lamp standard, and in five minutes there'd be a line of people waiting to be seen."

"Fiona, I know this is a sensitive subject." *Here it comes.* "You're over fifty. Have you met anyone lately? There's been no one since that Tim person. That was, what, ten years ago? I remember when you both came to visit. He seemed nice enough."

"Mom, it was twelve years ago, and Tim was a lazy mooch. And yes, I'm over fifty, closer to sixty. Most men want someone a lot younger." This subject was a grizzly bear with a sore paw. "Or they want a nurse to take care of them. So, no, no men. If and when I rope one in, I'll let you know."

"Honestly Fiona, I'm at the point that if you said you were dating a woman, I'd just be happy you weren't alone. Look at your sister. Two kids and married for thirty-two years."

"Yes, Mom." Fiona kept silent. There was nothing else that could be added to her mother's summary of her sister's success.

"Fiona, dear, believe me, I'm glad you found a job. I know you don't have much of a pension. I hope it's good. What is the position this time?"

Fiona wondered if her mother ever considered mentioning any of her good qualities. "I'll be working at a long-term care facility. It's night shift and some weekends."

"Isn't that a demotion? Do you really want to go back to working nights? You'll never meet anyone that way."

"I didn't meet anyone working in an office for the past eight years either. With my skill set, this is what I'm qualified for." Fiona felt she had summed up her lack of accomplishments quite nicely.

"Well, I hope you can stay at this one. You aren't getting any younger. By the way, when are you coming home?" her mother asked.

"I'm thinking of coming home next spring. I like Manitoba in the spring thaw." At eighty-six, Fiona's mother found travelling too difficult. Fiona had to go to her.

"What are you saying? No one likes Manitoba in the spring thaw. You couldn't come this summer? We could all spend time at the lake. You could get to know your nieces better. They're in their twenties now. They'll be married with their own kids soon."

"With my new job I need to accrue vacation time before I get to take any." Fiona waited for her mother to say something about how if she hadn't given up her hospital job twenty years ago to try a hand at a failed business venture making soap, she'd have a good pension, better vacation time, and all the other perks that it had come with.

"How's Heather and the family doing?" Fiona knew changing the subject to her sister's perfect family and her sister's perfect life was safer territory.

While Fiona sat, listening to her mother talk about her grandchildren, thoughts about her own disappointments surfaced. Fiona had always thought she'd get married, have kids, own a home, take family vacations to warm places, and spend time at the cottage. Yet, somehow, here she was, stuck in the life she was living. If getting up and going to work and coming home again was called living.

"Fiona, are you still there? You're awfully quiet."

"Yes, Mom. I'm still here." *Still here and going nowhere.*

Brice

Where's that ad? Brice felt like a spy looking for the secret code before the bomb went off. Frantically, he rummaged through his backpack. *What's this? A Watchtower?* Brice remembered being handed the flyer by one of the two ladies standing in front of the bank. He had no intention of reading it, but he hadn't wanted to hurt their feelings, so he took it. Reaching in, he found two pieces of balled-up paper. The first was the scrunched-up tissue he'd cried into after his talk with Dr Kapolian. The second was a liquor store receipt for two bottles of semi-expensive Pinot Grigio. One and a half of which he'd also cried into after his talk with Dr Kapolian.

Brice tipped his pack upside down. That ad had to be here. Unzipping the inner pocket, he shoved in his hand. *Found it!* He unfolded the Waterview Retirement Village ad, then opened his computer and typed in the website. There were three levels of care. The first was Azalea Tower.

All the special comforts of your own home without the worry. If you're looking for friendship, community, and a wide array of activities and events, it's here for the taking. Enjoy the safety and peace of mind that

comes with living at Azalea Tower. Meals and light housekeeping can also be included in your package. Ages 55+.

It looked lovely. There were pictures of people smiling into the camera, eating gourmet meals, taking trips to the casino, and playing rounds of golf. People having fun, living their lives independently. But it had to be expensive if you had to do a deep search for the price tag.

Next was Begonia Tower. Still independent living for the most part, Begonia offered help with medication management and medical appointments. They also offered in-house physio and occupational therapies. The folks in these shots looked much the same as at Azealia Tower, only most had mobility aids.

The last level of care, the one closer to the heavens, was Calla Lily Tower. No mention of independence here. Calla Lily was long-term care with some government-subsidized spots based on income. When his ALS worsened, a subsidized place like Calla Lily Tower was what Brice would need. Here they showed pictures of residents in the dining room, shots of people with an Elvis impersonator in a sing-a-long, and photos of the lounge area with residents playing board games, watching TV, talking to friends. At Calla Lily Tower the residents looked elderly. This was concerning. He was only fifty-five. Unfortunately, the type of help he would eventually need could only be found in long-term care. Unless of course you had money to burn and could afford to pay for at-home 24-hour nursing services.

Long-term care. Nursing home. Old age facility. He had been forced to think about such places when both his parents and then

Peter's father had to be placed. If Brice had ever entertained the thought about nursing care for himself, he would have said he had three good decades before he needed that kind of support. Now with his ALS diagnosis hanging over him, he found himself fiendishly searching the web for places he could go to when he'd need more help. Otherwise, he'd end up being placed in whatever long-term care facility was available. Brice typed the information into his phone then closed up his computer. He'd give them a call and get going on his plan.

"Nice to meet you, Mr Sanderson. I'm Mr Richards. But please, call me Kevin. No formalities; we're all family here at Waterview Retirement Village. First, let me apologize. I see I was mistaken. I thought this placement was for you. Are you the spokesperson for your family member? We usually meet with the person directly."

"You were correct the first time, Kevin."

"I'm not sure what you mean?"

"The apartment. It's for me."

"I don't want to appear rude, Mr Sanderson, but aren't you a bit young for such an arrangement?"

"Well, thank you, Kevin. Please call me Brice. By the way, it's been some time since I was referred to as young. But seriously, I find myself in the position of needing to move. I'm being renovicted after twenty years in my apartment. I'm not interested in buying anything at this stage of my life, and with the cost of renting these days, I may as well move into retirement living. To quote your advertisement, 'Waterview offers the freedom and independence to reach my dreams.'" Brice smiled, ready with his own sales pitch. "In all truth, I'm fifty-five. A fifty-five with joie de vivre, by the way.

There's so much Waterview offers—meals, light housekeeping, community. Have I died and gone to heaven, Kevin?" Brice only hoped Kevin wouldn't figure out the real reason he was wanting to move in—to get on the waiting list for Calla Lily Tower.

"Well, Waterview is a heaven for our residents. Still, it might be less expensive for you to rent an apartment. You could always have prepared meals delivered. And you could privately pay for cleaning services."

"I'm surprised you'd make such a suggestion Kevin. I'd have thought you would want my five thousand a month."

"Actually, we've just announced a price increase. But let's leave that to one side for now. We're here to offer the best options for each individual. We have quite a few people living here who are more than capable of living on their own. For various reasons, they look to Azalea Tower at Waterview Retirement Village. Maybe their partner has died or family and friends have moved away and they want the community and the amenities we offer. At Azalea Tower, residents have their own independence without the responsibility. There is no shortage of people looking to live with us."

Poop. Where did people get the money? At five thousand, he could barely afford a one-year stay. *The ALS better progress quickly.* Brice needed to get into the government-subsidized section of Waterview before his money ran out. "Kevin, are you discouraging me?"

"I hope I'm not. If this is really something you want to consider, please give us the opportunity to help. May I ask if you have any health problems?"

Was the man a clairvoyant? There wasn't a chance Brice was telling Kevin or Azalea Tower about his ALS. If he said anything, for sure they'd choose someone else who wouldn't start to drool or piss their pants. Brice only hoped that when he got to the point that he needed more care, there'd be a place for him at Calla Lily Tower.

Adelina

The heavy groceries made her arms feel as if they were stretched like something in a funhouse mirror. Opening the door, Adelina could see the laundry hamper overturned in the entryway. She set the bags by the door.

"Don, I'm home. Are you alright?" Adelina called out over the sound of canned laughter coming from the TV. She stepped over the dirty clothes into the living room.

"It's my back." Don, bowed like a pipe cleaner figure, walked toward her with his hand on his lower back as if to show he wasn't lying. "Call me when lunch is ready." He moved snail-like back to the couch. It had been a week since her layoff and Adelina needed to find a new job. Thankfully there was a small severance package to help for a few weeks. After that was used up, it would be onto unemployment insurance and desperation. Staying home these past few days had made her realize even more how little she and Don had in common. Their life together was like one of those Venn diagrams she learned about in school. Their overlap was debt, stress, and poverty.

Adelina put the groceries away before tackling the laundry left in the entranceway. She started dividing the clothing into two piles—white and colours. Don couldn't manage even that simple task. Adelina went through each piece as if chanting a meditation. Check pockets, turn colours inside out, separate whites. She thought of Joni. One time, Joni had been talking about how society had changed with men doing what used to be women's work. Adelina had laughed at that. Don would leave the laundry in a pile for her to pick up and sort, like he'd done today. Or when he'd clean the bathroom, he'd take out the supplies and maybe Windex the mirror and wipe down the sink. Then leave the rest for her. If he offered to make dinner, all Don seemed able to manage were omelets. In the end, it was easier for Adelina to do the chores. Once, she'd confided in Joni that it would be nice to come home to fresh laundry, a clean apartment, and a meal. But today Adelina didn't mind. The rhythm of separating the clothes and putting them into piles was soothing in its simplicity.

As she felt into one of her pockets, Adelina found the ad for Waterview Retirement Village that Joni had given her—she'd totally forgotten about it. *Joni.* What happened between them wasn't an ending. It was more like something hanging in mid-air. Adelina bore no grudge. She knew Joni, like her, like all the staff at Office Cleaning Services, had to watch out for herself. No one else would. Both she and Joni had been complicit in keeping the secret. How could Adelina harbour ill feelings when she had done the same?

There was a website listed for further information. But Adelina's only access to a computer had been to borrow Joni's when she brought it to work. Before Joni, Adelina would go to the library. A slow-moving snake, the line-ups crept along the outer wall of the library computer room out into the hallway. To meet the constant demand, each computer was timed to shut down after an hour.

Adelina would call the Waterview, take her resume down, and hand it in like the old days.

She put the separated laundry piles in the hamper. It was time to make lunch. Everything seemed to rest on her shoulders, and she was at the end of her rope. The rope she could either hang herself with or rappel down to make her escape.

Dressed in a blue jacket, a bright white tee, and casual dress pants, the man standing across the desk pointed to a chair. He looked about thirty-five, maybe forty. He reminded Adelina of a cologne advertisement in a men's magazine. Adelina doubted he'd ever been a housekeeper. *Those that do, do. Those that don't, don't.*

"Hello, Adele. Just like the singer. My name is Mr White. I'm in charge of the housekeeping and maintenance departments. Please take a seat."

"Thank you, Mr White." Adelina sat down. "My name is Adelina."

"Oh, yes. Right. Thank you. I wouldn't want to call you by the wrong name now, would I? I might get mixed up and give the job to someone named Adele." His smile was smarmy as he took the seat across from her. Adelina was used to this kind of behaviour. People in power didn't always care to know your name if you weren't important to them.

Mr White looked down at her resume. "So you're applying for a housekeeping position. Is that correct?"

"Yes. My most recent job was office cleaning."

"Office work is very different from cleaning peoples' rooms. There are many demands on your work day in a care facility. There is also bodily waste that needs to be cleaned up. How would you feel about working in those types of conditions?"

"Yes, Mr White. It does not bother me. I've cleaned medical offices."

"Here at Waterview Retirement Village, Calla Lily Tower, we are in the midst of a re-fit with some of our employees. We're trying to accommodate schedules and workloads. This means some of our workers have reapplied and are first in line for the daytime positions. Basically, only the night shift needs filling."

"That's fine Mr White. I'm used to working nights."

"Well now, that's great. Your references, by the way, are very good. Your supervisor Joni Howard gave you a glowing report. It says here that she was sorry to see you go. You worked there for eleven years?"

"Yes."

"What made you leave?"

Adelina knew this man would not want to know the truth about how the workers got laid off and then had to re-apply for their jobs for double the work. "I saw your ad in the paper. Waterview Retirement Village sounded like a good place that cared for the residents and the staff. A place where I would like to work."

"Wonderful." Mr White stood and extended his right hand. "Thank you for coming in today. My colleagues and I are meeting with a few others before we make any decisions. I'll get back to you early next week with an answer. On your way out, would you ask the next person to come in?"

Adelina wanted to wash off the slick Mr White. But she knew Don would be at the door waiting. It made him nervous, her not working, even for a few weeks. It made her nervous too. Their debt was quicksand, swallowing them up. Adelina rubbed her sore arm as she walked to their apartment building. When she'd gotten up to do the supper dishes the night before, Don had pulled her back down, forcing her to sit.

"What do you think your chances of getting the job are?" he had asked, as if she had a magic wand. Poof, you have the job.

But she knew Don was desperate. He was like a drowning man grasping at a lifesaver, but the line was too short to reach him. Growing up poor with parents who drank and gave him little love, Don had basically brought himself up. Embarrassed by his parents, worried people would see them drunk, Don made few friends. Once, when they first married and things were going well, he told her it felt as if he had stolen someone else's identity. That he never knew living could be so good or that he could feel so happy. Now the job, the house, his health, were all in the far-away distance. Only she was left. It was that poor little boy inside Don, by himself on the playground, watching the others, no one including him, that made her stay.

Adelina hesitated, then picked up the phone. It had been months since she'd called her parents or any of her three sisters in Calgary. It'd been even longer since she'd seen them. The last time was three years ago at the hotel her youngest sister Marina and her family were staying at on a stop-over on their way to an Alaskan cruise. Don hadn't come.

That last visit with her sister had made her family's absence all the more real to her. With so much distance and time between them, Adelina realized her parents and her sisters had become familiar strangers. Things between them hadn't always been that way. Growing up, her family had all been so close. After she and Don got married, they even rented an apartment in the same building. Everyone would have dinner together a couple of times during the week and on Sundays after church. They celebrated every holiday together. If anyone needed a hand, one of them was there to help.

Then, thirty years ago, her parents made the decision to move to Alberta. Her parents, in their late forties by then, added up their futures in Vancouver, and it came out to zero. But in Calgary word was you could get a good paying job, maybe afford a house, and take good vacations. Her parents joked that they'd get used to the cold. After all, they'd be able to buy a parka with the money they'd make—maybe two.

Her parents had hoped she and Don would join them. But those days Don had his good-paying union factory job, Adelina had her government job at the hospital cafeteria, and they had just bought their starter home. And so, when Adelina had gently asked Don if they could move, he put his foot down.

"Your family gathers 'round like flies to shit. Always doing everything together. I need my space. I was never so glad as when we bought our house and moved out of that apartment away from all of them. We're staying here." And since he was her husband and she loved him, they stayed.

Then, Don lost his job, Adelina got laid off when the hospital privatized her job, and they had to sell their home. They could no longer afford to take trips to Alberta to see her family, trips Don had never wanted to take. Her family, busy with their own lives, didn't get back to Vancouver very often. The few times they did visit, Don was not welcoming. Then, after a particularly high phone bill, calls were reduced to holidays, birthdays, and the occasional catch-up.

On that last visit three years before, Marina had taken Adelina aside. Their parents were concerned. Was everything OK? Adelina rarely called, and she and Don never came to see them.

"Please, Adelina," Marina had begged, "Come visit us. We miss you so much. Please, let us pay for your airline tickets. Any one of us has plenty of room for you both. Everything will be taken care of. Come."

But Don's "We pay our own way or we don't go" was the vice grip keeping her from visiting. Now when Adelina called, no one offered anything, and she didn't ask. All she knew was that she missed them and wished they were closer.

Fiona

Fiona stood at the door to Waterview's Calla Lily Tower, doing the math. Or more like an approximation. After tonight, she'd have only 2,549 night shifts to go until retirement. She balanced her blue thermal lunch bag with its contents of tuna fish on rye and a large, Suncrisp apple in her left hand. In her right, she held her stainless-steel water bottle. On it was a picture of a bent man becoming more upright, changing into a chimpanzee with each step. From her right wrist her purse dangled heavily under the weight of her most recent Margaret Atwood hardcover.

She pressed the code into the keypad, glad all she had to do was punch in a few numbers. At a workshop called 'The Future of Big Data,' Fiona learned that some places were using fingerprints and retinal scans as identifiers. The same talk warned that soon employers would be gathering DNA. As far as Fiona was concerned, everyone could have as much of her DNA as they wanted. When she was dead.

The intercom answered with a ringtone, then a voice spoke to her: "Hello, you've reached Waterview Retirement Village, Calla Lily Tower. How may I help you?" Surely, they didn't make the receptionist say this each time? But the fact that the voice was asking, even to someone who had typed in the code, could be seen on the monitor, and hopefully knew where they were by the sign on the door, had to be more nonsense coming from some branding company.

Fiona lowered her face to the intercom. "I'm Fiona Waters, RN. It's my first shift."

"Yes, we're expecting you, Fiona. Welcome to Waterview Village. We hope you enjoy working with the Waterview family at Calla Lily Tower. Please take the elevator up to three and then follow the yellow line on the floor. Again, welcome to Waterview."

Fiona did as the voice said and, looking down at the yellow line, put her right foot in front of her left. She felt like Dorothy attempting to find the great and powerful Oz. Only, in place of ruby slippers, she was wearing her new, white duty shoes with custom orthotic inserts, and her beige, prescription support hose. Not exactly the kind of get-up you clicked your heels in three times to get yourself back to Kansas. But if they helped prevent tired, aching legs and sore feet, she was wearing them. Fiona stopped and looked up at the ceiling. She wanted to make sure there were no flying monkeys waiting to swoop down and get her.

When Fiona arrived at the nursing station, there was no one there to welcome her. She looked around. No one was coming. Being of a certain vintage, Fiona waited to be asked in. Something stressed in her nursing program as showing respect, like asking the captain of a boat permission to board. As she stood there, she listened. The low sounds of the night shift echoed through the dark. A call bell was chiming, a signal for help. Far off, the tinny din of an old radio kept someone company. The furnace shutting on and off turned heat into sound. A troubled moan from a cloudy consciousness called out, followed by a voice comforting, "Hush now. It's the nurse. I'm here." It had been years since Fiona worked nights and heard such sounds. She peered down the corridor. The dimmed lights created an amber glow as the ghosts of loneliness, despair, and death walked the hallways. Back when Fiona had worked night shifts, she often felt these ghosts moving alongside her, keeping her company. Fiona never knew why they were there. She'd been too afraid to look beyond their shadows.

Footsteps. Finally, someone was coming to greet her. The approaching person appeared to be about eighteen. Getting nearer, the young woman looked at Fiona, then went into the nursing station and stood behind an opening in the plexiglass window. "Can I help you?"

I was just looking around. Don't mind me. "Hello, I'm Fiona."

"What can I do to help you?"

"I'm here to start my new job."

"Oh, I remember hearing someone new was starting. I guess that's you."

What else would anyone be doing here at 10:35 p.m.? Fiona stepped one imaginary foot up and onto the high road. "Yes, that's me, Fiona Waters. Registered Nurse. Starting the night shift. Tonight. I'm here for orientation."

"Welcome, Fiona. I am Sarah. With an h. I'm one of the evening nurses. I leave at eleven." Two minutes into their conversation, Sarah-with-an-h was already announcing her imminent departure. With no further conversation, Sarah turned her back and walked over to the opposite desk.

"Can you show me where I need to go?" Fiona asked, startled by Sarah's lack of assistance.

"Not really. I need to finish my charting so I can leave on time. Margaret, your co-worker, will be here at eleven to orient you. Please have a seat."

Sarah-with-an-h, sat down at the desk and picked up a silver, metal patient chart. There was no further conversation. There wasn't even a let me show you the fridge so you can put your tuna fish on rye away." No "here's a nice cup of coffee while you wait." No "take off your coat and hang it here."

Fiona came into the nurses' station and took a seat. With her coat on, she placed her lunch bag, water bottle, and purse on the desk. Fiona made a mental note of her thoughts and feelings. She learned to do this at the 'Better Morale at Work Starts with Me' seminar she'd been sent to a few years back. No way was this first impression making for good morale.

Her back still facing Fiona, Sarah stood and pulled her cell phone from her pant pocket. *What was it with people and their cell phones?* Sarah was too busy to take five minutes to help Fiona get settled but could take all the time in the world to sit there texting away? Fiona's thoughts returned to retirement. Freedom fifty-five. You never heard that retirement plan advertised anymore. Not even from Mike, the insurance agent that used to sell it. Fiona had recently run into him at the grocery store. At 62 Mike was still selling insurance. Only now he sold policies to snowbirds heading to warmer climes.

"It's very lucrative," he'd said to her, standing over the chicken thighs in the meat section. "No one wants to get into some unforeseen medical crisis without insurance coverage—it'd break the bank. Here's my card. If you're ever thinking of taking a trip, call. Number's right on the front."

In the distance, a shuffling noise interrupted the nighttime hum. There might have been a scraping sound too. Fiona couldn't quite make it out. *Surely Sarah heard it too?* Fiona looked at Sarah's back. She'd put her phone down and was now writing something in the metal chart, still not bothering to look up.

Fiona knew that sound, or its lack, told a nurse so much. Slippers padding down the hall would let you know someone was up at 3:00 a.m., and why. A bang could mean someone had fallen. A toilet flushing and then a bang might indicate someone had fallen on their way back to bed. Laboured, irregular breathing was a sign that a patient was having respiratory difficulty. If the laboured breathing was new, it was an emergency. If the laboured breathing was old, it was a signal death was waiting. Someone sobbing could mean pain or loneliness or loss. A call for mother, in a nursing home, indicated dementia; in a children's ward, fear.

The sound, closer now, was hesitant. One—two. One—two. Was that a swish? Sarah, not even an ear cocked or a glance upward, kept writing. Why wasn't Sarah doing something? The person obviously needed assistance. Fiona was about to get up when the one—two, one—two came to a stop. Fiona could hear heavy breathing behind her.

With a low, night-nurse voice, Sarah said, "Hi, Margaret. How did you sleep?"

Fiona turned. A woman looking older than Fiona entered the station. Fiona made a quick nursing assessment—Margaret owned a pair of arthritic knees. Both burdened by excessive weight and probably in need of replacing. Fiona could only guess they were painful which made it difficult for her to lift her feet. The swishing sound in all likelihood was caused by the carry bag. Hung from

Margaret's wrist, it more than likely hit the wall with each step as she held onto the railing. The laboured breathing, well that could be from a number of health conditions. Being out of shape was the most obvious. It could also be that Margaret was a smoker or ex-smoker, either resulting in lung issues. Or, assessing the age factor, it could be heart failure. Fiona would need to see both ankles for swelling to rule out that diagnosis. Sarah turned around.

"Margaret, let me introduce you to Fiona, your new co-worker, here for orientation."

Two things came instantly to Fiona's mind. First, Margaret, hopefully, was on a knee replacement list. Second, if Margaret was her work mate, those 2,549 remaining night shifts were going to be very long ones.

Brice

At the entrance to Azalea Tower Brice stopped to catch his breath. Long before his diagnosis, Dr Kapolian had told him he needed to improve his cardiovascular fitness. "You're out of shape, Brice. Very out of shape."

At the time, Brice had argued that his laboured breathing was due to stress. "I heard about it on the CBC," he told Dr Kapolian. "'Shallow Breathing and the Never-Ending Cycle of Stress.' You should listen to the podcast. It's very informative."

Now, with ALS looming over him, Brice wished he'd taken exercise more seriously. Going into ALS in better shape, muscles stronger, could only help.

Brice inhaled a deep breath. Then let his head fall back. Exhaling, he looked up. The sky was visual poetry. All pillowed and white and floating above him were pockets of clouds against the robins' egg blue sky. *I look at clouds from both sides now. From up and down and still somehow...* Good old Joni Mitchell. A perfect angel drifted above him, its wings spread. He read somewhere that an angel in the clouds was a message of love from heaven. Brice's balance shifted. He brought his head down to keep from falling. When he looked up again, the angel had turned to wisps like something drawn with a feather. Brice wasn't sure how many skies he had left to see. He breathed in deeply again, then offered up a word of gratitude to the heavens. He entered the code into the pad, each finger press intentional and determined. A few moments later, a voice came over the intercom.

"Hello. Waterview Retirement Village, Azalea Tower. How may I help you?"

"I am Brice Sanderson. I'm here to sign my contract."

"Ah, Mr Sanderson, we are expecting you. Please come in and follow the green line through the lobby to the manager's office. She'll be there to greet you."

The door opened slowly and Brice went through it. His life as he knew it was behind him. Below his feet lay the long green line he had to follow.

Adelina

Adelina walked past the front two buildings before arriving at Calla Lily Tower. It was as if she were a teenager starting another new school. Would she like it? Would they like her? Would she like them? Would she make friends? When she found Office Cleaning Services, Adelina had hoped that would carry her to retirement. But you never knew God's plan. Adelina bent her head in a quick prayer. *God, please let your light shine through me.* Washing floors and cleaning toilets might be looked down upon by some as menial tasks, but Adelina knew that no matter how small or unskilled the task was, in everything there was God.

Adelina pressed the keypad. "Waterview Retirement Village, Calla Lily Tower. May I help you?"

"Hello. I'm Adelina. I'm here for my new position in the housekeeping department."

"We've been expecting you, Adelina. Welcome to Waterview. Please come in. Walk straight ahead to the bank of elevators. Take the freight basement. When you get off the elevator, follow the blue line on to the housekeeping department. Oh, and welcome to the Waterview family." A buzzing sounded, and the door opened.

At the elevators, Adelina pressed the down button and the

doors opened up on a large elevator car. She climbed in and turned to face forward. Adelina pressed the B button. It seemed to her that the housekeeping and maintenance departments were always housed in basements. This arrangement kept the lowest-level workers away from the professionals on the upper floors.

The elevator came to an abrupt stop and the doors slowly opened. The basement lights were bright white compared to the dimmed upstairs lighting of the lobby. Adelina blinked—a mole coming into the sunshine. She followed the blue line to a set of automatic doors. The sign above read, "Housekeeping Department. Please stand back. Doors open outward."

Adelina stepped back, took a deep breath, then spoke into the intercom. "Hello, it's Adelina Warren. I'm here for my first shift."

"Stand back. I'm opening the doors," a voice boomed back at her as the door opened onto a large open area. To the left, a woman wearing a dark blue uniform was emptying a bucket of dirty, sudsy water into a deep sink. Another woman, also dressed in the same blue uniform, was lining up two housekeeping carts. These carts were the same no matter the building—office tower, hospital, hotel. At the back end of each cart, a large, oblong ring held a heavy canvas bag lined with plastic for garbage. At the other end, standing soldier straight, lived the mop and broom. The bottom shelf had space for cleaning agents, rags, a bucket and a dustpan. Sometimes cleaners, to save time, would put their lunch bags there. A half-an-hour break went too quickly when you found yourself waiting for the elevator to get to the fridge for your lunch.

The two women turned to her. "Hi, I'm Holly," the woman lining up the carts said as she came over, her hand outstretched.

Blonde, brittle hair with indigo streaks; fragile-thin, chicken-bone legs; Adelina guessed the woman was either a young-looking forty something or an old-looking thirty. "You must be Adelina. We'll be working together. This is Gloria. Gloria does the evening shift."

Adelina looked over at Gloria. A scrunchy was doing its best to keep her dark brown ponytail in place. Streaks of grey indicated a lack of time, money, or concern about getting her hair done. Gloria looked to be in her early fifties. She carried the abdominal weight middle-age brought with it.

"Hi," said Gloria, putting her now empty bucket on the bottom shelf of her cart. "My partner Joyce already left. I'm cleaning up for her." Gloria wiped her hand on her uniform before extending it. Adelina shook her hand. It was sandpaper rough. "We do that sometimes. Help each other out." Adelina was not sure if this was said to inform or challenge.

"Nice to meet you both." Adelina looked back and forth at each of them. She sent a quick prayer to God that Holly would be a good partner.

"Well, ladies," Gloria said, gathering up her coat and purse. "I'm out the door. I think you'll enjoy working here, Adelina. We all came to the conclusion that it's better to work together than not. Helps us all get along." With that, Gloria pressed the button and the doors swung outward. She walked out without a look back.

"Let me get you started, Adelina. First, here are your uniforms." Holly handed Adelina a brown paper bag. "They give us two to start. You sent them your size, I hope? Not that any of us will be walking the catwalk in Paris wearing them. The bathroom is over there."

Fiona

Fiona trudged to the bus stop yawning, her head down as if holding it up took too much effort. Poor Miss Mosely in 305, she needed continual monitoring before the on-call doctor finally sent her to hospital. There had been little time to sit down or take much of a food break. Even so, after so many years of office work, it was a good feeling to be back to hands-on nursing. Still, the work was more tiring than Fiona remembered. Plus, she was that much older.

At bus shelters, Fiona made it a rule to stand. (You never knew who did what to a bench.) However, exhaustion had a way of lowering one's standards. She sat down and pulled the crinkled bus schedule out of her purse. Fifteen minutes. Her first night off after starting her new job and Fiona was planning a celebratory dinner that evening with Deb. Decades-long friends, they'd met during orientation to their first jobs on a medical ward. Had they really been that fresh-faced and perky? Hectic and busy, breaks often missed, they both worked hard. They played hard too. Fiona laughed to herself.

One time, just after starting their jobs, Deb went for drinks and woke up to find she had passed out under a bush on someone's front lawn. With only fifteen minutes until the start of her shift, up she got, peed behind a cedar hedge, brushed the grass off her uniform and came into work. On-time. Deb worked the whole eight hours too, tired and hung-over, with the other nurses pulling grass from her hair all day long. That story became legend. God, did they have fun.

Fiona yawned. She thought of cancelling their plans. Getting used to working nights wasn't easy. It might be just as nice to sleep as late as she could and then hang out at home in her pyjamas. Plus, Fiona wasn't sure if she was quite ready for Deb. Like a woman who splashed on too much cheap perfume, Deb could be overpowering. It wasn't Deb per se that got to Fiona. It was Deb's life. Retired at fifty-five with a great pension, Deb was travelling, meeting men, trying new things like paddle-boarding and pickleball. Meanwhile, Fiona's earliest retirement date, if she wanted any kind of a pension, would be more like seventy. Fiona's life consisted of going to work and sitting at home. Alone. This didn't offer up much in the way of exciting conversation.

What reason could Fiona give to beg off? Headache. (No, Fiona used that excuse last time.) Stomach upset. (Used that the time before the last time.) Diarrhea. (In the past Fiona used this one so much that Deb insisted Fiona get a colonoscopy.) This time when they made their plans, Deb had warned, "No cancelling, Fiona." Deb wanted to fill Fiona in on the new man she had met. (What happened to the last one?)

Fiona only hoped their evening wouldn't turn into an I-told-you-so get-together. *Fiona, if only you hung in there like I did, you'd be retired with a full pension. Fiona, your issues with authority have only ever gotten you into trouble. Maybe you should try not saying what you really feel. Fiona, if only you'd swallowed your pride, you'd be married, in management, anything but where you are now.*

It was hard for Fiona to admit, but sometimes, in Deb's company, she felt like a big, fat loser—a less than. But it was a chance to get out and feel alive. Go to a restaurant. Enjoy dinner cooked by someone else. Have a glass or two of wine. And who knew, maybe it would be like the old times when she and Deb just laughed.

Brice

Brice looked around his new one-bedroom. Heck, a 500-square-foot condo in a bad neighbourhood of Vancouver could set you back $350,000 minimum. Meanwhile, here he was, four hundred square feet with his own bathroom, bedroom, living area, and a small kitchenette. All for the grand sum of $5,500 a month. Food and light housekeeping thrown in. Picking up his yellow-handled exacto knife, Brice was glad to see his grip steady. *Surprise me.* Brice cut into the clear, plastic packing tape. Any hopes of labelling his boxes had gone after he lost his black Sharpie, which he fully expected to find in some other packed-up box. Folding back the flaps and removing the packing paper, he dove into the box. Things were indeed looking up. His plates were there, washed and ready for the shelf. They'd be even better when he found his food. (Meals were covered at Waterview, but he still might want to make a little something in between times.) Brice looked down at his rounded stomach. From his experience with Peter wasting away, he knew it helped to have some extra meat on the bone.

There was a knock at the door. Brice opened it to find a petite, perky woman sporting a stylish blonde bob. Dressed in a fashionable outfit of white cotton pants, an orange golf shirt, and blue sneakers. She reminded him of a window he had dressed last summer. The display had been quite the hit with its theme, "Sporting the Look." For that one, he had used gender-neutral, multi-racial mannequins. The brightly coloured clothes were accented beautifully by the various skin tones. Both customers and staff said the effect was amazing. A few gay meet-up groups gave it a thumbs up on social media. It didn't hurt that some made a point of buying a few of the outfits.

"Welcome. My name is Cassandra. But, please, call me Cassie. All my friends do. I've brought you a welcome-to-Azalea-Tower pie. I made it myself." Her outstretched arms regally presented him with a deep-dish pie. The aroma of cooked apples and cinnamon wafted up to his nose. She stepped into his apartment.

"Ah, thank you so much. I am..." What was he? Overcome? "I'm Brice. Thank you for such a wonderful welcome. I never want to meet a person who doesn't love pie."

"Especially apple," Cassie said, looking at Brice's exacto knife. "You aren't going to do me any harm are you?"

"Only if you want your pie back," Brice joked, putting his knife down. He took the pie from her. "Now isn't this a dainty dish to set before the king?"

"It's a small gesture. I want to make you feel at home. Especially being as young as we are. We youth have to stick together."

How old was she? Maybe mid-to-late sixties? "I'm a great lover of the apple, especially when housed in a light, flaky pastry. I hope I can return the favour."

"Well, I'm sure you can, but I can see you're in the middle of unpacking and I must be off. I'm going to hit a couple of buckets. The activities are one of the reasons I moved here. That and not being ready to be alone after my divorce." Cassie added, matter of fact as she looked around the room. "It's been a year and a half since I moved in. You should join me in a hit sometime. Have you looked at the list yet?"

"The list?"

"The activity list. There's so much to do here if you can get onto the list. Keep this one on the quiet," she said, her boisterous voice taking on a decided whisper. "I sign on before I go jogging at 6:30."

"I can do 6:30. Is that before or after supper?"

"Brice, you're so cute. 6:30. In the morning."

Brice came to a quick realization. If he had to get up before the sun, he might never get to see the list. Forget about signing up for anything on it.

"It used to be online, but to make things fair, they've made it a first-come, first-served hand sign-in sheet. It's at the entrance to the common room."

"How's that fair?"

"People can get quite heated when something is especially popular. When it was online, people were sitting up until midnight to sign up. The same people booked everything. Words were said. Not nice ones either. Some people are still not talking. Well, I must run." Cassie looked down at her watch. "Let's catch up later."

Closing the door, Brice looked around his apartment. He needed to get down to some serious box opening. So far, he'd opened a total of two. Brice turned to a box labelled kitchen U's. Brice opened it to find his forks, knives, and spoons. "How wonderful!" He pulled out a fork from the box. "I don't have to be a philistine to eat my pie." Brice hoped his sense of propriety would stand him well into his illness when his faculties were on the wane.

When the next knock came, his first thought was, *Please don't let her want her pie back*. But this time, standing before him was a salt-and-pepper, wire-haired woman holding a plate with a cake cover. She wore blue jeans and a loose-fitting, black T-shirt over her unharnessed, sagging breasts. Two cats in a sack, his dad would have said. Not politically correct, but accurate. White block letters on the front read, "I'm menopausal. Don't bug me." Brice looked down past her offering. As he expected, she was wearing Birkenstocks. One saving grace, no socks.

"Hi, I'm Barbara. I've brought you a cake. Chocolate. I thought I was safe with chocolate. Everyone loves chocolate. You do love chocolate, don't you?"

Two of the universal truths as far as Brice was concerned: everyone dies and everyone loves chocolate. "I do believe you are correct in that supposition, Barbara."

"Well, I wanted to meet you. It's not every day a man moves in here. By himself, I mean. I'm sure you'll be bombarded by all the women creating a stampede to your door. There are so many desperados here, Brice. Be careful, they will do anything to snag a man."

Like making a chocolate cake? "Thanks so much for the warning. I appreciate it."

"I see you are in the midst of unpacking. Such a chore."

"Yes. Chore." Did anyone like unpacking? A no-fun activity as far as he was concerned. Packing wasn't all that great either. "Needs must. I just found the forks. Good thing!" He nodded to the cake she had placed on the counter.

Quietly, Barbara had maneuvered her way over to his La-Z-Boy and sat down. She pulled the lever and leaned back.

"So Brice, what's your story?"

"Story?"

"You know, a young man such as yourself moving into Azalea Tower?"

"I could ask the same thing about you, Barbara." He guessed her age to be late sixties, early seventies.

"I asked you first." She was making some serious eye contact.

"That's true. You did." Brice started to feel like he was in a staring contest. He looked away.

Undeterred, Barbara continued. "So, Brice. What is it?"

Brice found his mind wandering to thoughts of high school dances. Everyone trying so hard to look cool—all positioning themselves around everyone else. He'd go with his female friends as the someone-to-dance-with-if-no-one-asks-me guy. It worked for both sides. They had someone to dance with and Brice got to keep up the pretence he was straight. He'd wondered how gays were accepted at Azalea Tower. But he had held back from asking during his interview. Brice hoped people at Waterview Village were enlightened. However, the demographics were the age range that some of his past tormentors would be now.

"Barbara, can we talk about this once I get my unpacking done?"

"Ah, hiding something, are we?" It was exactly like the school dance. Only served with cake. "Alright, Brice. You're busy. I'll leave you to it. Maybe I will see you at dinner. Do you know what sitting you are down for?"

"Sitting?" Brice asked.

"Oh, you're not on the meal plan? I know a lot of folks here make their own food. But I find it easier to have my meals prepared for me, so I pay extra for that. Works out to be about the same with less hassle."

"No, I'm on the plan." Brice started to wonder if he needed a scheduler for all this.

"Well, there are two sittings so they can fit everyone in. Plus, some people like to eat earlier and some later. If you head to the dining room, they'll let you know what time you're down for. It would have come in your package. You don't want to miss tonight. It's roast beef and Yorkshire pudding."

Besides apple pie and chocolate cake, roast beef and Yorkshire pudding were his two most favourite foods. "I never thought I'd have to decide on meal times. It sounds so scheduled. Do I get to pick?"

"I prefer the later sitting. Most of the younger people here like later, and there is only so much room. You might be on the early list. Unfortunately, that's when the older people eat. Not that there's anything wrong with being old. They like to be in bed by 8:00 p.m., so there's not much socializing with them after dinner. You can always sign the change-of-dinner-time list. Word of warning, it can take a while. You have to wait until someone moves out or dies."

Brice started wondering if Barbara was someone best to avoid. "There sure are a lot of lists that need signing around here."

"It might help if you read your package. You did get a package?"

Lists to sign and packages to read. Two of his not-so-favourite things. "The movers probably dropped a box on it."

"Or it came and you just didn't bother to read it. Most people don't read the package. Then they complain when they don't get what they want."

"When I find it, I'll read it. Until then, I have your cake and a deep-dish apple pie I can survive on."

"Apple pie! Don't tell me Cassie came by with her old stand-by. She probably had some bruised apples she had to use up."

"She was off to play golf."

"She's still playing golf? Oh, that is surprising."

"It is?"

"After what happened, it sure is."

"What happened?"

With that, Barbara hit the lever of his La-Z-Boy and sat bolt upright. She leaned toward him, her eyes gleaming in a conspiratorial fashion. He was reminded of a Halloween jack-o'-lantern. All that was missing was the candle. "I'm not one to gossip, but Cassie was doing the Netflix and chill with the golf pro."

"Oh." He nodded back at her. When he found his computer, he'd have to Google "Netflix and chill."

"That one spread all over the complex. No one understands how Cassie could actually think he was after her. He must have thought she had money. She doesn't, by the way."

Brice was beginning to think Barbara was more jealous of Cassie than she was sorry. He hoped Waterview wouldn't be like his hometown. Small. Gossipy. Everyone knowing your business and not minding their own.

"Well, Brice, let me know when you're done. We can have coffee. I'd love a piece of cake. It's my specialty. I'm just down the hall. Very end. This side. Name's on the door." Her eyes stared back at him.

He wondered if getting a piece of cake might not be the only slice she was looking for. "I'll probably be here unpacking for a while. Maybe days even. Another time?"

"Next time, then. You'll have to bring my plate back with something on it for us to share."

"You never know." But he did know. Of course, he'd eat the cake. Who said no to chocolate? After that, he'd keep his distance. He knew a piranha in sensible shoes when he saw one. Brice tripped over a box on his way to the door. Opening it, he smiled at Barbara.

"Ah, the universal cue to leave. Well, I accept your not-so-subtle hint, Brice. But I warn you. I'll be back to get my answers." Brice felt like he was back in school, standing before the principal.

A few boxes later, Brice noticed his hand was unsteady. He must be more tired than he realized. About to take out his shirts, Brice heard another knock. *This is busier than the Vancouver airport.* He got up to open the door. An older woman with straight, silver, bobbed hair, dressed in slacks and a shirt, stood at his door. She looked classic. He judged her age to be anywhere from 60 to 75.

"Hi, I'm Carolyn. May I come in?" Carolyn said, entering as she spoke.

"Hello, Carolyn." Brice extended his hand. "I'm Brice, and well, I think you are in already, aren't you?"

"Yes, I guess I am. What a mess," she said, gingerly stepping over one box and then another. "Just like a man. By the looks of things, you didn't downsize before you moved?"

"This *is* downsized." Brice shrugged his shoulders and looked around the room. "Looks like I need to do some more."

"By the way, I knew your name. We all did. We knew your age too. Round about anyway. And that you were moving in. Alone."

"Isn't that supposed to be confidential?" Brice asked, not certain if he should or shouldn't be upset with a breach of his privacy.

"There are ways. Besides, it's not every day we get a young one moving in. Most people are in the over-seventy range. But that's changing. Look at you for instance." Carolyn looked around. "Ah, I knew it. A pie and a cake. The welcoming brigade must have been by."

"The welcoming brigade?"

"Cassie and Barbara."

"Why, yes. How did you...?"

"They always get to the new man first."

"The new man...?" The light was beginning to shine down on him. He was the new man. The new available man.

"Yes, the women here are hungry, and you are the buffet."

"So that's why the desserts," Brice said, nodding to Carolyn. Alone in the clearing, he was prey. Circling above, the scavenger birds were waiting for a chance to dig their talons into his back and take him back to their nest.

"You're safe with me, Brice."

"Safe?"

"Yes, safe. I'm gay."

Safe. Gay. Together these were finger-on-the-trigger kind of words. Like a bloated body in deep waters, a dark memory surfaced. Distant and choppy, it played out in his head, like watching an old home movie where the film had snapped from the reel. Badly taped back together, some parts missing, the movements were jagged. For Brice this memory had always been difficult.

He'd gone with Noleen to his very last high school dance before graduation. Shy and sensitive, her personality outshone her ordinary looks. Great traits for a friend, not great for getting you an invitation to the dance. At the end of the evening Jay, a quarterback on the high-school football team, showed up. Alone. Brice had loved Jay since grade two, long before Jay became one of the most popular jocks in high school and only hung out with the cool people. That night at the dance, when Jay saw Brice, he averted his eyes. Then, drew them back again. Mystery lived in Jay's look. (Why now?) Subtle moves were at play. (Signifying, what?) Jay, coming up to Brice at the punch bowl.

"Hi Brice. How ya doing?"

Brice stammered back a hesitant, "Good."

Brice had been shocked that Jay was actually speaking to him. Then, the warm whisper of Jay's breath on Brice's face as Brice, hands full with drinks, tried to pass by. Later, when Brice headed to the boys' room, Jay followed behind him. Brice could still feel the burn of hot water as he slowly washed his hands to prolong leaving. Anything to find out what Jay wanted. Desired. The sound of Jay moving behind him. Jay's reflection in the mirror looking over Brice's shoulder. Brice turning around as Jay stepped in closer toward him. Brice's face upturned to meet Jay's. Then the sound of fury. Unleashed, it came thundering in.

Football players. Laughing. Mocking. "Look at the fairy." The captain. "Gotcha now, you little faggot." Chokehold to a bathroom stall. Brice's head rammed into the toilet. The feel of cold water swirling around his head as the toilet flushed. The smell of urine and feces as it got into his eyes and ears and mouth. The feel of boot to back. Such betrayal. Worse still, the feeling of never-ending shame was a black shadow, following him even now. Always waiting.

"Brice. Where are you?" Carolyn asked, a look of concern on her face. "I haven't scared you, have I?"

Brice shook his head. "Not at all. Just good to know I'm safe with you."

Carolyn looked at him (in a knowing way?), but hadn't he been tricked by knowing ways before? Hadn't he done that by believing Jay loved him back? Before he said anything about his sexuality to anyone, Brice needed to be sure. The cruelty of such an act all those years ago was a ghost that still haunted him

Adelina

Walking out into the morning, Adelina gave thanks to God. She was happy. Waterview was going to be a good place to work. Holly was going to be a good workmate. Holly not only explained things, she helped with the work. Often when Adelina started a new job, the person showing her around decided it was like a day off. They did nothing except call out orders and point to the things that needed doing. Not Holly.

Holly had been with the Waterview organization for five years now and had explained that, even with the recent changes, the benefits and pay were some of the best in the industry. Adelina had never heard a housekeeper talk this way before. Words like organization and industry were words Adelina associated with professionals in offices, not broom pushers like them. Holly told her most staff were proud to be working there.

If the Waterview benefits were as good as Holly said, Adelina might be able to finally afford better medications. Her diabetes was well controlled now and she wanted to keep it that way. But for her, that also meant more expensive drugs. It seemed so often the way with the poor. Even for those needing something as essential as medications, many had to choose food and rent over paying for pills. So often in her life she felt like a beggar finding a small coin on the ground. A coin most people wouldn't bother themselves enough to bend down and pick up. But to folks like her that coin made a difference. It was the same way with fair wages and benefits. So many took these for granted, but for the poor, they were everything.

In the quiet, waiting for the bus, Adelina's mind turned to Don and their first meeting. It had all started out so differently. A couple of years after finishing high school, she'd met him at a church dance. He'd looked so handsome. Handsome to her anyway, with his ocean blue eyes and wavy, sandy brown hair. Shy, alone, new to the church, Don stood across the room looking her way, before finally coming over and asking her to dance. Six feet tall, he towered over her, making her feel protected. Now his height frightened her. They met up a few times after that. Always at church and with others. For privacy they would step outside and take a walk in the church garden.

As the relationship became more serious, Adelina told her parents. "Prospects," they told her. "A man who believes in God and has a good job? Adelina, you won't do any better than Don." He proposed five months later. Their wedding was held in the church basement. Friends and family brought the food. Within a year they had saved enough for a down payment on a small home on the Vancouver-Burnaby border. Thirty-five years ago, if you made a good wage, that area of town was affordable. They were able to get ahead, too, until the factory moved and Don's union job went along with it. His new job had paid half the wages, and the company's safety measures were poor. Then Don got hurt.

When the government privatized her hospital cafeteria job

and the new company cut wages and benefits, it spelt disaster for her and for her co-workers. Few knew, but there had been suicides, divorces, children pulled from school because their parents weren't able to afford the tuition. People's lives had been broken. The government said it was to save money, but it was corporate greed.

Soon after, both their hard-earned savings dwindled. Still, they got through it. "We ain't singing the blues, we're living them." Don joked when he still had a sense of humour. Then, somewhere in the midst of all their anguish, Don turned his back on God and before long there was no space left in Don for love. Drink filled him instead. And that was when the monster had come to stay.

Adelina couldn't keep thinking this way. Not on such a fine morning. The past was over. The sun was shining. Seven days in at her new job and she was feeling truly blessed. God was watching out for her. And even though Joni had not answered her calls, Adelina prayed Joni was happy in her new role. People didn't always understand. To not forgive was a sore that kept festering. Adelina wanted no part of such a wound.

Fiona

Saying a cursory hello to the one other person waiting at the bus shelter, Fiona moved to the opposite corner and sat down. They'd been introduced on what turned out to be each of their first days at Waterview. Already Fiona had forgotten the woman's name. Adelaide or Adeline, something like that. Fiona didn't want to appear snobbish. It was just that, after working a nightshift alongside Margaret, she didn't feel like small talk. "Hello," was the best Fiona could muster. Last night on her one-month anniversary Fiona had tried to have the talk with Margaret.

"I've been here for a month now, Margaret. how am I doing?"

"How are you doing?" Margaret asked, looking up, somewhat perplexed. "I don't know. How are you doing?"

"I mean how am I doing at my job? When will you be giving me my evaluation? Ways I can improve." Fiona learned to ask for feedback at an 'Asking for Feedback' seminar she once took. It could be quite the shock to think you were doing well only to find out you were the only one who thought so.

"That's management's responsibility. I'm just helping you settle."

"Margaret, I think in order for them to know how I'm doing,

it needs to come from the staff with whom I am working. That would be you."

"Well, yes, in a roundabout way. It could be me."

"You're the only RN I work with. How is management going to know how I am doing if you don't tell them?"

"I never really gave it much thought."

This was not a surprising response. So many things seemed not to be Margaret's job, including Margaret's job.

"Margaret, for all they know I could be an axe murderer."

"I don't really think they'd care if you were an axe murderer. As long as you show up for work," Margaret joked, looking down at her phone. "I know it hasn't been easy getting a nurse to work nights. Or, for that matter, an axe murderer."

Just when did the standards get so low? In the past, if you didn't answer the call bell in a timely fashion—three rings—you'd be given due warning. If it happened again, you were suspended. Now, according to Margaret, you could chop off someone's head on your day off and, as long as you showed up for work, all was good. Fiona would have to come up with another plan for getting a performance review. And she'd have to tell Margaret about her own job performance. Margaret seemed to think looking at her grandkids' faces on Facebook every three seconds was part of her job. But it wasn't easy trying to say anything to Margaret. In the face of all her infirmities, Fiona felt heartless bringing up fair workloads.

Margaret's list of ailments was endless. "It's my bunions. Both feet tonight. I feel like I'm walking shoeless on a Mexican beach in July," Margaret told her at the nursing station, shoes off as she rubbed one foot and then the other. Another night it was her hemorrhoids—which Margaret shamelessly reported were like sitting on burning embers. A constant complaint were her painful knees—both of which needed replacing. Margaret was planning to get them done before she retired. She wanted to use up her sick time and get paid for her convalescence. "But I have sleep apnea. That puts me at a higher risk, so the waitlist for surgery is even longer." Margaret told Fiona this as proudly as if she'd won an award. Some nights, Fiona wished she were an axe murderer.

Brice

One month in at Waterview and finally his shoulders felt like they weren't around his ears. "How about you, Shammy? Enjoying your new home?" Brice had picked up his shamrock the week before at the hardware store. One aisle over from the home décor section, a roll of two-sided hanging tape in hand (hammering nails into the walls for your pictures wasn't allowed), somehow Brice had ended up in the plant section. He believed this act of fate was thanks to his great-great-grandfather Shamus. Irish. Never met. Long-departed. Amongst the shamrock's leaves, a few dainty white bells made a valiant effort to flower. Not an easy feat amidst the bright lights, dry air, and flagrant neglect of the gardening section. Its flowers made him think of small trumpets signalling hope. So he'd brought the shamrock home and put it on his half-table under the window.

"We're a team Shammy. You get a better life, I have company." Whenever he looked over at the plant, Brice could see its green-burgundy leaves. They spread themselves out in the morning seeking the sun. At night they closed in tight on themselves. The circle of life.

Brice opened the kitchen drawer. After a poor night's sleep, he'd slept in and missed breakfast. Not that he minded. Today was a be-by-yourself kind of day. Brice loved being alone. It was something he'd started doing more and more since Peter's death. Friends called, but Brice rarely answered. It was as if when Peter died he took people-loving Brice with him and left behind loner Brice. It had been months since he even looked at Facebook.

He lifted the frying pan to get at the griddle. Of all the things he packed, the griddle reminded him most of Peter. It was one of the few things Peter had received when his mother passed (the distribution of Peter's mother's belongings having nothing to do with fairness). After the funeral, when Peter finally made it over to his mother's house, his sister Mary, who had packed up the family home, presented the griddle to him like it was some rare artifact. But in the end, it turned out to be a most precious gift.

For Brice, pancakes were a taste of the past. His most lovely past with Peter. Every Sunday Peter would hold up the griddle like it was a tennis racket and pretend to serve a tennis ball over the net. (Funny thing, neither of them played tennis.) This was the official signal Sunday brunch was starting. Apron on, disco music up, griddle on the stove, Peter would make his to-die-for-pancakes and sausages. They'd drink a pot of coffee (sometimes two), pour gobs of maple syrup over everything, eat until stuffed, and leave the dishes for later. Then they would read the paper, make love, nap, and laugh. How could Brice not hold onto such a keepsake? It was a memory holder.

"But even still Shammy, I'd have loved the Limoges."

Brice looked about again at the empty boxes, used packing tape, and paper stuffing strewn about his apartment. He closed his eyes, then opened them again. *Still there.* He hadn't expected settling in would take so long. Some of the delay was because of the events he couldn't resist signing up for. With a deadly, debilitating disease hovering over him, Brice needed to make the most of the time he had left. *Who could say no to murder mystery night?* Or a trip to the casino. Or appetizers and wine pairing night. Or a talk on local fauna. (Admittedly, that one was to avoid unpacking, but at least he'd learned something.) And he hadn't counted on how the changes in his health would affect him, slow him down. He'd go to put something on a shelf. It would drop from his hand. He'd walk over to empty a box. Then he'd trip over his foot. There were days his muscles ached with fatigue. Brice made another appointment with Dr Kapolian.

Cane. Walker. Wheelchair. Bed. Swallowing difficulties. Soft food. Feeding tube. Respiratory decline. Breathing mask. Loss of speech. Tracheostomy. Ventilator. Infection. Die. Blunt as ever, Dr Kapolian had laid out the ALS trajectory of his illness and his likely death. At least that was how Brice heard it. Dr Kapolian had looked over at Brice. "Am I scaring you?"

No kidding after that list.

"I say all this not to frighten you, but to acknowledge the obvious. With your changes—feeling more fatigued, losing your grip more often, and tripping over your feet—it might be time for you to consider getting measured for a cane."

"A cane?" Brice had asked, hearing his deepened voice. It was almost as if someone else was talking.

"Something to consider for the not-so-distant future, Brice. It's hard to hear all this, I know, but it helps you make plans for the future."

"Doesn't sound like a future I want to have, Dr Kapolian."

"I've learned that, when it comes to dealing with one's health, it's best to have a plan of action before it's needed. When nothing's been put in place it's just mayhem and confusion trying to get things in order."

"Thank you, Dr Kapolian." *We're dealing with my death here. Should I be calling him something less formal? Dr K?*

"Beside the declines you have told me about, have you noticed the timbre of your voice? It sounds deeper and a bit raspy. A sign of ALS worsening."

"Maybe I'll get to sound like Darth Vader," Brice joked.

"I'm ordering you a sleeping pill. I know you've said you're sleeping well right now. However, I anticipate with the stress of all of what is happening to you and with some of the future symptoms such as muscle cramping and restless legs, for example, you may just need them. I want to make sure you have them on hand. They'll help on those nights when you can't get to sleep. They're usually for the short term, but in your case, well, the truth is, addiction doesn't matter. Sleep does. I'm also going to refer you to an occupational therapist for the cane fitting and a swallowing assessment. We want to make sure you're able to swallow your food without any problems. Plus, it's a good idea to develop a relationship with an occupational therapist now. You'll need them more and more as the disease progresses. Have you thought about getting your estate in order?"

"I only have my sister left. And a few, not so gay-friendly second cousins I'm estranged from. I don't have much to leave really. *Here goes.* But there is something else that I would like to discuss. Something I have been wondering about. Since we're talking about getting plans in place."

"Yes?" Dr Kapolian looked up from the prescription pad.

"Do you remember with Peter when he asked you about medical assistance in dying before he died? But it was illegal then so he couldn't do it."

"Yes, I remember. We were able to get Peter the supports he needed as he required them. When I went to see him that last time in hospice, he told me he was comfortable and getting good care. You were able to be with him when he passed, if I recall?"

"Yes, I was with him every day. They gave me a cot on the floor beside his bed. I got to be there right beside him when he died. But, Dr Kapolian, it won't be the same for me. I have no one who can care for me like I did with Peter. Plus, with short-staffing and more people in need, I hear home-support in the community isn't as good as when Peter used it. I'll have to go to long-term care to get help or wither away taking up resources in a hospital. And, well, I'm not sure how to say this, but now that MAID is legal, I'm thinking it might be something for me to consider. Just in case things get too painful and difficult. You know, before I die." Brice looked at Dr Kapolian hoping a smile might debut. But lately Dr Kapolian had only two looks—serious and dead serious.

"Brice, I didn't know you were thinking this way. I still believe there are many other options we can put in place. Many people with ALS live at home with support. We can get things put in place at your new residence—when the time comes. There's also hospice."

"So no need to go all Sue Rodriguez right now?"

"Ah, Sue Rodriguez. That was such a long time ago. More recently, there was the Carter case. Do you know about that?"

Brice shook his head. "I remember seeing her on TV. She was

fighting for the right to die with MAID, wasn't she?"

"Yes, she was. In 2015 Kay Carter and another woman, Gloria Taylor, challenged the law denying assisted suicide. The law was subsequently overturned, and MAID became legal. Although it's still a small percentage of deaths, I do know more and more people are opting for it. Brice, I need to tell you, as a Catholic, I'm not involved with the MAID process. But I am your doctor, and I will help support you in whatever way I can. I believe there are other ways to help people living with terminal illness. But you have the right to your decision. I just don't think you're at that stage right now."

"No, Dr Kapolian, I'm not. I want to keep it as an option. Just in case."

"Maybe you should do some research on it, and I will too. There have been some changes to the regulations around MAID since 2016. I have had a few patients choose to do it without my knowledge. I only found out after they'd gone ahead with it. I'm glad you confided in me. We need to work together. Thinking about such a decision on your own can't have been easy, let alone talking it over with me today." Dr Kapolian headed to the door and opened it. "Here's your prescription for the sleeping aid. Please speak to Nurse Winworth on the way out. She'll book another appointment for you in a month. If anything changes, please call."

Brice headed to his pre-booked cab. Sue Rodriguez had been relatively young when she was diagnosed with ALS. Her case happened in the early 90s. Brice hadn't paid much attention to her fight for the legal right to die because he'd been too busy with the fight to live. The AIDS epidemic had devastated the gay community for over a decade by then. Brice had been protesting for access to drug treatment, housing, food security, and to stop discriminatory practices against people with AIDS. He and Sue might have been fighting different battles, but they were both fighting. Not successful, she had ended her life illegally. Now, in part because of Sue Rodriguez's courage, he was able to legally seek medical assistance in dying.

Brice got into the cab. *Thanks, Sue.* The cab slowly pulled away from the curb and joined the traffic

Adelina

Adelina gathered up her purse and coat. Time to go home. Walking to the front exit, Adelina thought about her first month working at Waterview. It wasn't the same as working with Joni—eleven years couldn't be replaced in a month. Still, it was good. She thought back to that last day only a few short weeks ago. Everyone lined up to receive their packages like people waiting in a soup line. Funny, that morning felt so remote and distant—like looking through an old album and seeing yourself in a photo. A photo of a time you didn't remember, let alone the people beside you. So to get a better look, you lifted the album closer to your eyes. But the moment once captured was long forgotten. And as you put the album back down, all you could think was how, once, it must have been important for you to have saved that picture. For there you were, young and smiling out from the lower right-hand corner of the photo, surrounded by other smiling faces from your past.

Joni. If Adelina was honest, maybe there was no friendship left to save. They were like a divorced couple. Too much stuff was in the way to find resolution. Joni got promoted and Adelina lost her job. Neither of them had been completely honest with each other, and that was what true friendship meant—being honest.

"People from work are just that. People from work," Don had said to her, his smile exaggerated, his eyes wide from the drink when she first told him she had lost her job. "They don't care about you, Adelina. They only care about themselves. I'm your family. Not them. Not anyone else." Don was her family. How many times had he said this to her over the years? Words that were supposed to be comforting. Instead, they made her feel like she was living in setting cement.

It had often surprised Adelina that some of the residents were still awake when she got to work close to midnight. Some stayed up late reading. Some waited for family or friends in different time zones to call. Some, sadly, walked the halls, looking for sleep as if it had been dropped on the ground and all they needed to do was to pick it up and take it back to their rooms. "Might as well wear myself out rather than just lie there, dear. Walking might help me get back to sleep," they said to her as they held onto the railing.

Adelina loved connecting and engaging with the residents, even if it was only to ask, "How are you," "Do you need the night nurse," or "Can I do something for you?" But the resident she got to know best was Professor Moody in room #307. Adelina didn't know why Professor Moody was in Calla Lily Tower. He seemed too vibrant. But it wasn't for her to pry. Most nights, he was up when she started work and went to bed in the wee hours.

"I'm a tiger, nocturnal. My hunt is for knowledge. In the daytime there are too many predators out on the prowl," he joked. "Sometimes I get up in time for lunch. I don't want to miss too many meals since I pay for them. But some of the nonsense I get from the folks around here—I can miss out on that quite nicely." A retired professor of biology, he'd never been married or had a family. "I've always been solitary."

The professor shared many interesting ideas and research with her. Last night he told her about a PhD candidate who had discovered a new species of bird. The week before, it was an entomologist working in the American Southwest who found an insect thought long extinct. "These species survive because of evolution and not coming into contact with mankind, Adelina." He had looked directly at her, an equal.

Afraid such a learned man might ridicule her, she still stood by what was in her heart. "I believe in God's plan, Professor Moody, not evolution."

"And I respect your convictions, Adelina. I, too, believe there is a plan for the world. I'm just not sure who runs the show," he'd said. "It's your break soon. Why don't we go to the bistro and share a pot of tea?"

That was how the ritual started. Adelina would join him on her break and they would have tea together and talk. He never laughed at or patronized her. He accepted her. It was a shame that not everyone could be this way.

Even Holly disappointed her. One night while looking for Adelina, Holly had found her talking to Professor Moody. In front of them both, Holly turned to Adelina. "It's late. He should be in bed. The night nurse will be angry, Adelina."

After Holly left, Adelina apologized. Professor Moody only laughed. "Please don't let it worry you. People think if you go for a walk around here at night, you have dementia and can't find your room. Mine's right over there," he said, pointing in the wrong direction. Then seeing her shock, he laughed and nodded in the right direction. "Fooled you."

Adelina often wondered how much knowledge was lost to the world when no one listened to the old or the poor or the uneducated. These marginalized tribes of people often had no voice. Adelina knew what happened to your soul when no one listened. Over time it got worn down like rocks beaten by the pounding ocean.

When Adelina arrived at the bus stop, that nurse was there. Fiona. They had been introduced on her first night. Now, one month later, although they had stood at the bus stop many times since then, little more than a hello was said. Adelina was used to this. So often no one knew her name. They just knew she was one of the housekeepers. What made life like this? She was a good person. She did her job. She paid her bills. She did her best.

Adelina trudged onto the bus. Don had promised to do the supper dishes. Hopefully they were done. Now if only he'd make his own breakfast so she could wash up and go straight to bed.

Fiona

It was the start of Fiona's two days off from work. As the #20 bus drove by the liquor store, Fiona looked out the window. Should she wait fifteen minutes until the 9:00 a.m. opening? Coming home from work in the morning and stopping off at the liquor store on the start of her days off was becoming routine. Soon they'd be calling her by name. But after her meeting that morning with Christine from Human Resources, Fiona was flummoxed. Not only did she deserve a glass of wine with dinner, she needed one.

"Fiona, we all have our strengths. And yes, we all have our weaknesses. Margaret has been here for twenty years. She's one of our most valued employees. The residents love her." Christine said this while glancing down at her appointment book and flipping a page. Looking up, eye to eye with Fiona, she added, "You've been here three months now. I'm not sure why you aren't able to take your breaks. Or why you're getting off late most mornings. My takeaway from this is that there are areas for improvement we all can work on. Let's concentrate on those." Christine paused.

Fiona, not knowing doublespeak for "Margaret needs to pull her weight and do her job," said nothing.

"Waterview offers some great online courses. There's one on

time management you can take." Christine had handed Fiona a brochure. Just how "Margaret's not doing her share of work" was Fiona's time management problem, Fiona didn't understand. She was about to ask this when Christine closed her day timer, picked up her briefcase, and pointed the way out of the office. The management brush-off hadn't changed.

There was a new paradigm in the workforce that had Fiona feeling like she was in a maze she couldn't get out of; the walls were too high to see over and the path too convoluted. With no map to guide her, Fiona was lost. Maybe it was an age thing; her brain was too old to comprehend. Or the earth was turning too fast on its axis for her to keep up. Cancel culture had gone mad with everything needing a positive spin even when things weren't positive. How could you, them, or a situation improve when something was deemed good that wasn't? It didn't make sense. Not everything in life could be turned into a positive. That's what made life life. Shitty things happened. You had to pull up your bootstraps. Take the bull by the horns. Make lemonade out of lemons. Soldier on. These sayings weren't made up for nothing.

Maybe I'll buy that wine when I get up. Go for a walk. Get some exercise. Being in line when the liquor store opened was Fiona's own private signal that she had moved from wanting to needing. That was never good. On the other hand, it would be nice to have wine chilling in the fridge, ready to be poured while she heated her frozen pizza. Alcohol was not the answer, but more and more she was finding it helped her cope. A hard day at work? Glass of wine. An easy day at work? Glass of wine. Fucking new-age conversation about her lazy co-worker with a supervisor young enough to be her daughter? Bottle of wine.

Fiona needed... What did she need? Something new in her life? But how did you even do that at her age? Move. Join a walking club. Take up painting. Get a job in a field totally different from nursing. Something fun. Light. Carefree. She'd been a nurse supporting people with their illnesses, grief, anger, sadness, pain, and loss for thirty-five years. Everyone looked to the healthcare provider to be the old stalwart—always there to say something meaningful, therapeutic, or caring. Meanwhile, providers themselves were often overwhelmed by all the suffering and expectations, left feeling like a building ready for demolition, being imploded from the inside, not always able to say the right thing.

The bus stopped in front of the bagel shop and Fiona got off. *Would you like some cream cheese on your multigrain?* Beside it was Black Dog Video, one of the last DVD stores in Vancouver. She liked movies; maybe they needed someone? Not that she had any retail experience. But she could always learn. DVD stores always seemed to have people working in them who were on the fringes or in the arts, or a bit of both. Her turn to be one of those people. *I could dye my hair purple. Wear a funky rooster brooch on my shawl. Get the Chinese character for "good luck" tattooed on my left forearm. On my right, in ancient Greek, I'd put directions for getting red wine stains out of carpets. If anyone asked, I'd tell them it was Aristotle's motto on how to live a good life. The joke's on you, pal.*

She crossed the street and walked over to the liquor store. The lights were on; staff were behind the tills preparing for their day. She looked around at the others waiting at the entrance. It always surprised her when she wasn't the first one in line. Alcohol was not an innocent beverage. So many problems were related to it—cirrhosis, cancer, heart failure, pancreatitis, depression, sleep interruptions. Hell, the list made you want to have a drink. Fiona watched as a liquor store employee came over and unlocked the door. She fell into line, waiting her turn to cross the threshold and buy her bottle of salvation.

Brice

"Well, Cassie, I know you love golf, but all that walking just to get a ball in a hole—where is the joy?"

"It's more than getting a ball in a hole. It's about skill. It's about patience. It's about coordination."

"It's about frustration if you ask me." Brice laughed. "And I still have my foot problem. I'm still waiting to get an orthopedic surgery referral. Golf isn't in the cards yet. Soon, I hope." Brice wondered how long he could use his foot as an excuse to get out of things.

"Trust me." Cassie grinned. "When you get your foot taken care of, you'll learn to love golf. It's addictive."

"Golf, addictive? Chocolate is addictive. Cigarettes are addictive. Booze is addictive."

"You forgot sex. You've been here three months now. Just once, I would love to see you swing your club."

"Now Cassie, keep talking like that and I'll think you're flirting."

"Well, maybe I am?"

God no. This was not good. Brice had worked up his courage and tried to have something of the same conversation with

Barbara. He'd made some attempts to work his gayness into the conversation. The one with Barbara seemed to be recurring and endless. "Well, Barbara, most of my relationships with women were really just friendships," Brice had told her, feeling confident she'd catch on to what he was inferring.

"What about the ones that weren't?" Barbara had asked.

"I never had any of those."

"You poor thing. Life can be so cruel. We all need love."

"I haven't found love with a woman I..." He had started to tell Barbara he was gay when she interrupted him.

"It's never too late. Look at me; I am sure I've told you the story about me and Big Jerk?"

At times like this, when someone was about to repeat the story of their bad marriage, their failed love affair, the reason they don't talk to their family, their lazy-no-good kid, their botched nose job, their ex-spouse, could a person ever truly say, "Every chance you get?"

"Big Jerk and I loved each other once. I've no idea why but we did. Until the day we didn't. I'm still a romantic. Who knows, maybe you and I will both find love when we least expect it."

Three months at Waterview and he still hadn't told anyone he was gay. All his life, people had figured it out before he had to say anything. Did he have to start professing his love for Celine Dion for them to catch on? Brice knew he'd have to say something soon. But he needed to be certain. Institutions might stick a rainbow flag on the wall, but sometimes that could be for optics only. Waterview had one. It hung in the games room alongside flags of the world.

Waiting his turn at the shuffleboard, Brice had overheard Jeff, a new resident, ask, "What country is that from, Bob?"

Bob, a man Brice considered enlightened after learning he once attended a gay wedding, joked, "Somewhere in Africa."

"Very funny, Bob," Brice had interrupted.

"Is it from the Caribbean? They have such colourful flags," Bob answered, smiling.

"Funny again, Bob." Brice wondered if Bob was as enlightened as he first thought. "It's the universal acceptance symbol of the lesbian, gay, bisexual, transgender, and queer community."

"Accepted by whom? Not me." Bob laughed. "Let's set up this board. Brice, you're up next."

Having faced this kind of prejudice all his life, Brice was still hesitant to let people at Waterview know he was gay. He'd heard too many stories of homosexuals in long-term care not getting the help they needed. The care aides not wanting to look after them, as if being gay was something contagious they could catch. Many of the aides were from countries where homosexuality was looked down on, or worse, banned, and gays were jailed. How were these caregivers to turn off their beliefs just because they came to Canada? But having someone refuse to touch him, bathe him, lift him, or feed him when he needed help was not an option. One hoped this kind of thinking had stopped. Listening to Bob that day, Brice was reminded that it hadn't. It'd taken him so long to get out of the closet in the first place; now here he was, pretending once again to be something he wasn't.

Adelina

"Hi Holly, did you sleep well?" Adelina checked her cart.

"Five hours. As usual, I could'a used nine but my daughter brought the grandkids over. She needed to run some errands and there's no one else to leave them with right now. Her husband's working out of town again. The life of a long-hauler driver." Holly, yawned. "Oops, sorry."

Adelina stopped working and looked over at Holly. "Your daughter is very fortunate to have such a good mother. Your sons too." Holly's two sons still lived at home and she often helped with her daughter's children. It was no small wonder she was tired.

"You're right about that. There was no one for me to call for help after Steve ran off with his girlfriend. Guess that's why I help out. I know how it goes. I love my kids, but sometimes I wonder what my life would have been like if I hadn't married so young or had three kids by twenty-two. I was a child myself. Never once did I think I'd be a grandmother at forty-two. How'd you sleep?"

"Not good. Don was't feeling well. I slept on the couch." Adelina put her hand on her lower back and stretched. "It's not the most comfortable."

"You're working, Adelina. It should be him on the couch, not you. He seems to do that a lot."

"Don needs the bedroom when his back is bad."

"Well, you need to think about yourself. A poor sleep and then having to work hard isn't good for you either."

Adelina changed the subject. "Today is my three-month anniversary. I guess my probation is officially over." Adelina planned to stop by the church after work and say a prayer of thanks.

"I'm glad it's been good for you. And I'm glad you came to work here. With all the staff shuffling, working short all the time was killing me. None of us ever got paid any extra for it. We just got a few thank yous, and thank yous don't pay the bills. Guess they realized you can only work a donkey so long and hard before they dig in their heels or keel over."

"I'm so glad for the residents that the owners realized their mistakes."

"Don't kid yourself. When people pay lots of money for care, they don't want to see clouds of dust bunnies floating down the halls and no one answering the call bells. It wasn't until the families started threatening to move that management started hiring more cleaners and care aides. They can't get money from an empty room, now, can they?" Holly headed off to get the polisher.

Every week they took turns—one of them polishing the floors and the other one cleaning the halls. Adelina took the elevator up to the first floor. Stepping out into the amber lighting of the hall, a memory of Don bending over candles at the dinner table came to her. Now candles were not in their budget. Neither was romance. Taking out her rags and disinfectant spray, Adelina quietly started wiping down the hand railings. The motion soothed her. She thought of how she and Don had deeply loved each other so long ago. Now basic tolerance was getting difficult. Adelina stretched her back. She would start saving for a new couch. A beam of light fanned itself out from under Professor Moody's door. If it was still on when she got down that far, she'd stop for a chat.

From behind, Adelina heard the laboured wheezing of Margaret.

"Hello, Adelina." Margaret stopped, out of breath. "Mr Williams in #312," she continued, "had another accident. The aide got him cleaned up. However, he had some difficulty getting to the bathroom in time. Do you mind? It needs to be cleaned."

"Yes, nurse. Right away," Adelina said to her retreating back. Poor Margaret. Her knees were such a bother. Adelina hoped the hospital would call her soon so she could get her operations.

When she got to his room, Mr Williams lay there moaning. "Hello, Mr Williams. It's Adelina. I'm here to clean your bathroom. You sound uncomfortable. Can I get the aide to help you?"

"She just left, but thank you. I'm sorry. I missed the target, as it were. This, getting old..." He stopped.

"You know that's what I'm here for, Mr Williams. Please, don't be sorry."

"To think I owned a thirty-million-dollar-a-year company. Now they tell me I need to wear a diaper. Adelina, whoever said life would get easier was lying. Getting old and infirm is no way to live." Mr Williams looked up at the ceiling.

Adelina moved over to the bathroom with her rags and her pail. A few nights a week she was coming in here to clean up—poor man. When Adelina was finished, she'd stay a few minutes to talk. If Mr Williams wanted. Sometimes it was nice to have someone to tell your story to, someone to see you as more than just an old man who messed the bed, someone to remind you of who you once were. Adelina knew this all too well.

Summer/Fall 2019

Fiona

Four a.m.; the puking hour. A time when a person should be in bed—not wandering down some hall, flashlight in hand, doing hourly rounds on the residents, searching for calamity. As Fiona turned the corner into the next corridor, she wondered just how much longer she'd be able to do this. Living her life upside down. Turned around. Day, night. Night, day.

Fiona had come to terms with the fact that Margaret was never going to change. It must have been so much easier in Roman times when you could throw a lazy bugger to the lions. Although, getting a lion and finding a colosseum might take some work. Maybe she could use an angry bear in the woods to finish off Margaret and her bad knees. Tonight, however, she didn't mind doing the lion's share of the work. (What was it with all these lions?) Moving kept her mind off Professor Moody. She had been surprised to learn he'd died unexpectedly two days before, during her days off. Or as unexpectedly as you could die when you were eighty-one and living in long-term care. A diet aide had found him when he hadn't come to supper. He was sitting in his chair in front of his desk, a biology book open and a pen and writing pad beside it. Professor Moody was lucky. He died doing something he loved. Fiona hoped his last thoughts were good ones.

She opened the door to check on Mr Williams and pointed her flashlight downward. If you had dementia, a bright beam of light waking you up would seem like an alien invasion. Poor Mr Williams; his decline had been quick. All curled up and sleeping, he looked like a little boy. At least sleep gave him relief from the torment of losing his memory, losing himself. Fiona gently closed the door and started back on her rounds. Turning into Corridor D, and the door to Professor Moody's old room. Fiona thought about her own death. One thing was for sure, no way was she dying sitting in an easy chair, her last breath taken before the TV. When it was her turn, it was going to be her grand finale. J-walking across a busy street in Rome and being mowed down by a Vespa. Tumbling to her death after tripping over a loose rock at the top of the Acropolis. Dying from a brain hemorrhage after having fantastic sex with a young man not quite thirty-five. Definitely not dying in an old folks' home where they hardly waited for your bed to get cold before they moved the next person in.

Fiona entered Professor Moody's empty room. Her beam of light shone on the paint cans, brushes, and plastic sheets left by the painters readying for the morning. The label on one of the cans read seafoam green. Whatever colour seafoam green was. It was just nice that the person moving in was going with something modern sounding. So many of the residents seemed to pick something neutral. Or maybe it was picked for them. Shining her light on the walls, Fiona hoped seafoam clashed with everything. Old age was bland enough. Everyone, staff included, needed a reminder that they were alive and not just waiting for the grim reaper to reap.

Making her way back down the hall, Fiona looked in on the

other side. Just as expected, Miss Price, one hundred and one, lay on her back, sheets up to her neck—propriety, still the order of things, even in bed. Miss Price swore that sleeping on her back reduced her wrinkles. "You should try it," she'd advised after Fiona had mistakenly woke her up by leaning over her to see if she was still breathing. Really, would any middle-aged, sleep-deprived nurse leaning over your bed look good?

But Professor Moody was someone Fiona would really miss. She rarely got to speak to the patients except to say, "Let me help you get back to bed," "Here's a sip of water," or "Yes, the clock does say 3:00. But it's 3:00 in the morning and, no, you're not late for afternoon tea. Let me get you a biscuit if you're hungry." Up reading into the night when Fiona did her checks, the professor would tell her about his research. Or, as he called it, his time professing. Browsing his name, Fiona found all kinds of awards and accolades. Every comment made him sound like a favourite teacher, a supportive mentor, a long-time friend. That was before old age and infirmities landed him in Building C. Even he was loath to call it Calla Lily Tower. "It sounds pretentious." Professor Moody had told her.

Fiona wondered how Adelina would take the news. More than once, Fiona had found them chatting over tea. On the rare occasion she and Margaret got off work on time, Fiona would see Adelina at the bus stop. Mornings not her thing, Fiona said little more than hello. Then on rounds one night, Professor Moody had asked Fiona to join them. Looking down at the biscuits and tea, thinking about her other option of spending time at the nurse's station with Margaret commenting on her Facebook posts, Fiona had happily pulled up a chair.

Those had been such wonderful conversations: world events, upcoming celestial sights in the night sky, art—classic, modern, post-modern, whether bike lanes were a good thing. Fiona: no. Adelina: not sure. Professor Moody: a firm yes. Those wonderful discussions were the highlight of Fiona's nights—conducted while drinking herbal tea and munching on digestive biscuits. Fiona learned herbal tea was not just left-over flower tips some granola entrepreneur threw water over. (The exception: chamomile; to Fiona, that would always taste like drinking soap.) Not wired after great gobs of coffee trying to keep herself awake, Fiona was now sleeping better than ever when she got home from work. So now they'd sit together talking until Fiona's stop. Adelina's trip then continued east on the Skytrain. Then one more long bus ride to the outer edges of the lower mainland. Adelina's journey each day to and from work humbled Fiona. Both of them were so tired at the end of their shifts. Then poor Adelina had such a long commute to get home.

Fiona hoped she and Adelina would still meet up on their breaks—a Professor Moody legacy. She headed back toward the nursing station. Margaret was there just as Fiona had left her—head down, both she and her computer in sleep mode. Fiona slid the button on her flashlight off. Quietly, she entered the nurses' station and sat down.

Brice

Brice looked into the bathroom mirror. It reflected back at him a Brice desperately in need of seeing his hairstylist, but it was getting harder for him to get in to see Sebastian. His waitlist was long and Brice could only afford him every two months (a visit to Sebastian cost a small pay cheque), and it had now been over three. But his real reason for not getting his hair done? It was getting to be physically impossible for Brice to go anywhere on his own, even with the cane, occupational therapist Lisa advised.

A basic T-handle, Brice had really wanted the brass horsehead model. "Lisa, if you're going to go, go in style," he'd told her when she told him the practical reason for her recommendation (it was easier to grip). Practicality losing out to pride, Brice got the T-handle, in carved faux ivory—his personal aesthetic was still a priority.

Taking the bus was out of the question. If somehow Brice was able to make it to the bus stop, would he get a seat? His physical vocabulary no longer included standing and balancing. Brice could hear the bus driver's directive over the intercom. "If you're sitting in the handicap section and you aren't, please give this man his seat. Thank you." Then Brice would wait as one shamed, able-bodied person stood, their stolen throne reluctantly relinquished. Then, too, the very act of paying the bus fare would be a nightmare. Brice could barely grasp his Compass card, never mind swipe it to pay. If he used coins, for sure his toss would miss the fare box.

Brice didn't feel comfortable asking his friends for help either. Some he still hadn't told about his illness (vanity was a wall to climb over) and he could just imagine the ones he had let know. "Sure, Brice calls us...when he needs something." There was truth to this. After Peter's death, Brice had kept pretty much to himself. By choice or by chance, he wasn't sure. All Brice knew was that, since Peter died, his world had grown smaller. Now, with the shadow of his own death hovering over him, Brice's world was close to disappearing.

Of course, there were those friends who would always be there to help. Many called to keep in touch after Brice moved out of the West End—even folks from his old building. But few had cars to drive him; the West End was so walkable, and it cost so much to keep a car. Even he had given up his car after Peter's death. Others worked and wouldn't be able to get the time off, or they had their own health issues to deal with. So Brice cabbed it. Alone. That was the worst part of this whole ALS thing. The isolation.

A couple of attempts later, Brice had the T-handle of his cane in his weakened grasp. He moved away from the mirror, his steps unsteady, like a young child learning to walk. Slowly and carefully, Brice made his way over to the couch. The moving boxes were land mines scattered across the floor. Only six months ago they'd been packed and unpacked. Now here he was on repeat, moving to Calla Lily Tower. He felt like Bill Murray in *Groundhog Day*. Only with boxes. Luckily there was someone from the cleaning staff to help him—for a fee.

Awkwardly, Brice lowered himself, using his cane for balance. *I wonder how long my long-term care will be?* But like an elastic band about to break, Brice had stretched out his money paying for Azalea Tower and had little left. He didn't know what he'd have done if the government subsidized room hadn't come up. Even knowing his health was declining, only recently had he truly faced up to the fact that he needed the health support that Calla Lily offered. Brice looked around his room again. Even with his merciless cull, he still had a lot of boxes. Boxes that needed filling. Boxes that were filled. Boxes to donate to Big Brothers. Boxes for storage. Boxes on the kitchen counter. His life was in boxes. His death would be too. *Comes in pine.* Brice looked up at the sun coming through the window. It felt nice on his face, like a warm kiss.

His meeting a few days prior with Theresa, the Calla Lily Tower manager, had gone well. Theresa had given the requisite number of kindly nods. She maintained eye contact. She even had a box of Kleenex on the table. The tissue poking out reminded Brice of a set sail as Theresa outlined his navigational path. "We have packers for situations such as yours. They do try to get things done as economically as possible. If you can go through your belongings and sort out what to take, that helps bring your costs down. Do you think you are able to do this? Physically, I mean?" Theresa looked at Brice.

"I think I can. For the most part." It hit him that maybe he wouldn't be.

Theresa continued. "Question. Do you remember what the

rooms look like? You'd have been given a tour when you first came to Waterview. We do try to give a tour of all of our buildings. To get a feel."

"Well, that was six, seven months ago. To be honest I was focusing on Azalea Tower, then. Not my final resting place."

Theresa, the consummate professional, ignored his small joke. "I have the floor plan and a few photos of the room. Right now, it isn't accessible. The cleaners are busy with it. I could ask a resident with a similar layout if I could show you their room so you could get a better idea, if you like." She said this while laying out the map and photos on her desk. "See"—Theresa pointed to the pictures fanned out on the table— "there's a surprising amount of space. There's room for a wheelchair too." Theresa must have seen the look of horror on his face. Hastily she added, "Not that you'll need a wheelchair anytime soon. Of course."

Like a woman lying about her age, Brice had been avoiding the truth. Of course, he'd eventually need a wheelchair, like his uncle Jim. It was just that ignoring the fact made it seem less real. If Brice were honest, he could use a wheelchair on occasion now.

"See, there's even a tub." Theresa had moved on to the bathroom. "It's one of two rooms on the third floor that has one. Most rooms have showers only. It was also designed to have enough room for a lift."

"A lift?" Brice asked, not sure he wanted the answer.

"It's what moves you into and out of the tub. When you need it, of course. Not before." Then, back-pedalling, Theresa added, "Not everyone needs a lift, mind you. The last resident didn't. The care aide can give you a bath in your own place. Otherwise, you would go to the tub room at the end of the hall for your weekly bath. This room has everything to make you as comfortable as possible. You're very lucky this room has become available."

Brice felt the tears falling onto his cheeks. "I don't feel lucky. I'm sure the person who died isn't feeling all that lucky either." He leaned over awkwardly and pulled up on the tissue sail, removing it from its mooring.

"Waterview understands. This isn't an easy time for you. But decisions need to be made. I'm sure you can understand our position. There are people in line, waiting for both the room you currently occupy at Azalea and the one you are considering at Calla Lily."

"I feel like I'm on an assembly line that's moving too fast."

"It is fast. Let me go through the steps. Your new room is being readied now. This is Tuesday; the packers can come Friday to help you pack up. They'll do the physical move on Saturday. You'll be settled in Calla Lily Tower by Saturday night. Waterview will put the refund on your current room at Azalea Tower toward the part of the payment for Calla Lily that is not covered under government subsidy. I have to be honest with you, Brice. You only get this first right of refusal because you're already a member of the Waterview family. The provincial government will be looking at their waitlist of long-term care residents needing subsidized housing. If you don't say yes soon, it will go to someone else. I hate to be so blunt. But that is the truth." Theresa's voice softened. "Why don't we give it until after lunch for your decision? You can pick out a colour for your room, should you decide to take it. I know this is a difficult decision."

And even though Brice knew he had to take the room, wanted

to take the room, doing so—saying yes—meant facing his truth. He was one step closer to dying.

"What happens if I can't decide on the colour so soon?" Brice asked, not knowing what else to say. Everything was so out of his control.

"Beige happens," Theresa said, a hint of a smile on her face.

"What do I do about the things I can't take?"

Brice learned there were lots of things he could do. Give them away. Try selling them online. Put up a "Things for Sale" notice on the bulletin board. For a monthly fee, there were storage units. Last resort, the dumpster.

Brice gathered his courage. ALS was not his fault. Yet here he was, having to enter long-term care at fifty-five years of age. He felt like an innocent man being sent to jail for something he didn't do. It might be difficult to hear the answers, but he had to ask the questions. "There are a couple of things I'd like to discuss."

Theresa's look showed concern.

"I'm gay. I've not always been open with my sexual orientation for fear of being ostracized. I have only recently let anyone at Azalea know. Although, to be honest, it turns out a few had already guessed." Brice paused. "I'm hoping that's not going to be a problem?"

Theresa shook her head. "No Brice, that's not a problem."

Feeling the silence and knowing their time was almost up, Brice gathered his courage to continue. "I understand facilities have non-discrimination policies, and that's wonderful, but if the staff hold beliefs that LGBTQ folks are dirty or go against God's commandments or whatever their reasons, they may not give the person the care they need. It might be that the care provider isn't even aware they're being discriminatory, their beliefs are so ingrained in them. Believe me, I know from personal experience, not everyone agrees with diversity."

"Brice, I know this is a vulnerable time for you and I thank you for being honest. Let me assure you again, your being gay isn't a problem. Our non-discrimination policy isn't just something we pin to the wall. Any acts of discrimination will not be tolerated. We here at Waterview treat everyone equally. Waterview doesn't ask people for their religious status, race, or sexual orientation, unless they care to share that with us. We also conduct many educational staff programs. These are not only related to nursing care. They also include courses on the LGBTQ and racialized communities, as well as the different religious affiliations of our residents. To be clear, my door is always open if you have any problems or concerns about how you or anyone else is being treated."

"Thank you, Theresa. That puts me at ease." Brice paused.

Theresa looked at Brice. "You mentioned there were a couple of things?"

"Yes, I know that the average age of the residents at Cala Lily Tower is about seventy-five. That's twenty years older than I am. Unfortunately, for someone like me who needs nursing care and will need more as my condition progresses, there were few options available other than long-term care. That's why I looked at moving into a nursing home in the first place. To get that care. What concerns me is that, more than once, I've listened to stories about younger people who've had to go into long-term care to get the help they need, and they do get the care, the physical care. However, there's little for them in the way of activities or stimulation. You know, food for the soul, the stuff that makes life life.

What accommodations does Calla Lily Tower make for those of us who are younger?"

"Please let me first acknowledge that it's not easy for anyone to be dependent on others. Ideally, it would be better for people, young and old, to live in community-based housing, or to have better support in place in their own homes. However, that's not always possible. To accommodate the need to house and care for people with various health issues, the government subsidizes a few of our rooms for people under fifty-five. I can't go into detail because of confidentiality, but, for example, people with conditions such as cerebral palsy, full paraplegia, or, like yourself, ALS. We do our best to offer some individual programming. But there are only so many resources and that limits us in what we can offer. We do rely on family and volunteers, but honestly, that isn't always enough. Please let us know if there is something we can help you with. Calla Lily Tower will do its best to accommodate your request."

Sitting on his soon-to-be donated couch, Brice thought back on his time at Azalea Tower. He felt like he was that kid in public school who only came for part of grade three and then moved away. No one knew them all that well, and they were soon forgotten. People at Azalea Tower still acknowledged him, but now that they knew he had ALS, something had changed. If Brice was in the elevator, people would say hello, then turn to read the bulletins behind the glass. If someone was ahead of him, they'd wave and keep on going, not giving him a chance to catch up. Any offers to join trips to the casino or for chocolate cake or to meet for coffee had dried up. Brice was surrounded by people. Yet he was alone.

Everyone had been accepting when he told them he was gay; although, Barbara seemed a bit put out. "Why couldn't you share this with me? I told you all about Big Jerk." He couldn't answer her. What had he been afraid of? Being gay was who he was to the core. Then one month ago, Cassie took him aside.

"Brice, this isn't easy for me to say. But I need to say it. A few of us have been talking. We want you to know we support you."

"What? For being gay?" Brice waited for the usual response that came with such a statement. "Of course, we accept you for you. Of course, we don't care who you sleep with. I've even got a cousin we used to call a little flighty." Then they'd usually add something along the lines of "as long as you keep it to yourself."

"No, don't be silly. No one cares if you're gay. What we care about is you. Let me just say it: they hold AA meetings in the Chapel at Begonia Tower."

He'd almost signed up for the meetings just to keep them from knowing the truth. Anything to keep himself from facing the truth. Saying he had ALS out loud made it real. Denial had been his safe place. In reality, his denial was a house of cards in a windstorm. He'd tried so hard to ignore his growing fatigue, the constant tripping, his reliance on the driver to help him get onto the bus on trips to the casino, dropping his weights at the gym. (Not good, considering they were only two-pounders.) Then when Cassie suggested AA Brice realized he couldn't hide things anymore.

He went to see Dr Kapolian.

"Based on how fast your current symptoms are progressing, it seems certain your condition started earlier than we estimated. I'm sorry. This is not the easiest thing to hear."

"So that means my demise will be sooner rather than later?"

"I can't say that exactly. But it is more than likely." Dr Kapolian's voice, usually so direct and confident, hesitated.

For the first time, Brice saw Dr Kapolian. Truly saw him. Hunched over, head down, Dr Kapolian embodied failure as if he were personally responsible for Brice's condition. In that one small moment, Brice realized that he'd shared more intimate details with Dr Kapolian than with almost anyone else in the world. Not only was the mundane shared—the physicals, immunizations, referrals for specialists, and all the other things that made for a routine visit to the doctor. But they had shared the momentous and life-altering—Peter's cancer diagnosis, then death. Now his ALS and his own impending death.

"Dr Kapolian," Brice, said quietly.

"Yes, Brice."

"May I shake your hand?" Brice realized he hadn't done this once in twenty years.

Dr Kapolian got up and came over. He held out his hand.

Brice grabbed onto it. "Dr Kapolian, I have been through more with you than I have with most people. Except for Peter. I want to thank you for all you've done for me and all you did for Peter. I hope you know how much you mean to me. How much you meant to Peter. I want to say it now, while I still have my voice. Thank you. Please don't worry about me; I've got it covered." For the first time since they met, Brice saw Dr Kapolian's jaw tremble.

Brice then got assessed for Calla Lily Tower. He called friends to let them know he had ALS and how sorry he was he hadn't kept in touch more after Peter's death. That it had all been so overwhelming. Even now. Then he told Barbara, Cassie, and Carolyn, "No, I do not have a drinking problem. I have ALS." Soon after that, their visits dried up. Both Barbara and Cassie had moved on to the new guy (it looked like Cassie was winning), and Carolyn had wished Brice well. Her partner of forty years had died from multiple sclerosis and Brice's condition brought back too many painful memories. Not that Brice blamed anyone. No one wanted to be reminded how close their own toes were to the grave.

Next, he contacted his sister Marcia. She knew about his diagnosis, but except for calls about their parents' condition when they were still alive or how Peter was doing after his cancer diagnosis, or how she was doing after her hysterectomy, they spoke mainly on birthdays and holidays. They visited each other even less. This time when he called it was to let her know he was moving to long-term care—the implication being that he was deteriorating—he reached her at her cottage. She could most likely book a flight out in a few weeks.

"Would that be ok? It's been such a hard year for me. I really need this time off. You'll be good till then, won't you?"

For this, he had set up Skype? "I'll try not to deteriorate any more until you get here, Marcia."

"I'll ask for a leave. I'm just not sure when I can get out there. Or how long I can stay. You won't have any men there when I visit will you?"

"Marcia, I'm moving to long-term care. Not a bathhouse. I don't even know if they allow overnight visits. Hell, Marcia, I don't even know if I'd be able to have sex anymore. Although, there might be a couple of moves I can still do."

"Brice, please. There's no need to be crude. By the way, did you know your voice sounds different?"

At the end of the conversation, Brice decided it was a good

thing he'd most likely be dead or close to it when Marcia finally came to visit. Then again, denial might be her house of cards too.

Brice surveyed his room—packed and ready to go. Was this all it came to? Boxes and a life measured in inverse relationships? His ability to hold onto things was decreasing. His chance of choking was increasing as his ability to swallow was diminishing. Soon he'd be down to pureed slop with a thickening agent. The worse his condition became, the better his chances of immobility and then death. Tears of deep sadness spilled from his eyes as he shakily leaned over and tried to pull a tissue from the box. Unsuccessful, Brice let his tears flow. Tears not only for himself but also for the poor man whose room he was about to take.

Adelina

Inside the service elevator, Adelina took time to read the announcements tacked up behind glass:

- **Please bring all equipment to the housekeeping office at the end of your shift.**
- **Please wring out your mops and place them in the washing machine after using.**
- **Please read the communication book for updates.**

Thank you,
Housekeeping Management

Why did these memos have to sound like they were dealing with children? Adelina could see why they put their sign behind glass. If not, for sure someone would write something not so nice on the sign. Maybe they should talk to the person not doing their job, not tarnish everyone else who was working hard.

Finally, the elevator door opened. Industrial white walls greeted her. It was always cool down here. Nice now it was the summer, but probably not so nice when the dead of winter came. A typical facility basement with none of the finishing touches of the upper floors. No mouldings, wainscoting, or hardwood floors. No one could mistake this basement for anything other than a basement.

Adelina got to the housekeeping department. She'd been looking at this sign on the door for six months now. There were times Adelina wondered what it would be like to work in an office, to wear nice clothes, not to be exposed to disinfectants and solvents that dried your hands and made them look and feel weathered and worn. To wake up to the sunrise, not to go to bed with it. Nodding her head to the ladies as they readied themselves to leave, Adelina looked for Holly.

"Don't bother looking, Adelina. Holly's called in sick again." This from Gloria.

"Did she say what was wrong?" Adelina asked, worried.

"They never tell you. If she doesn't get back soon, she'll find herself out of a job." This from Joyce.

"Well, God will see her through whatever is happening to her."

"God may see her through it, Adelina. But it might be better for you if he picked up a broom and started sweeping." Gloria nodded her head toward Joyce. "Isn't that right Joyce?"

"God is good, Gloria." It hurt Adelina when Gloria made fun of her beliefs.

"Good for what, Adelina?"

Ignoring Gloria, Adelina started to take off her coat.

"Holly waited until 9:00 p.m. to call in. No one could come at such short notice."

It was true; Holly was calling in sick a lot, and Adelina was left many times picking up the slack. Doing her own job was hard enough. Doing two, well, that was asking a lot.

"Oh, and Adelina," Gloria said, taking her coat from her locker, "Professor Moody passed away today. Sorry. I know you were fond of him."

"Passed away? What do you mean he passed away?"

"He died in his chair doing some of his research. Although what research exactly was anyone's guess."

Joyce interrupted matter-of-factly. "Adelina, could you empty the garbage in the games room? I didn't get a chance to go back there. I was busy with Mr Williams. The nurse asked me to clean his room. The poor man had another accident."

"But Professor Moody looked so good the last time I saw him," Adelina said in disbelief. They'd had tea and biscuits with Fiona in the kitchenette only two days ago.

"His room has been cleaned and the painters have their ladders and drop cloths in there already," Gloria said as she gathered her bag before heading to the elevator. "Nothing gets a chance to get cold around here. Dead residents or their rooms." A gentle rain of tears slowly fell from Adelina's eyes. Gloria turned back to Adelina. "Don't kill yourself trying to do two jobs. I know things are getting harder around here. If Professor Moody's empty room getting filled so fast is any indication, the bastards are making enough money."

Adelina thought about the last time she, Professor Moody, and Fiona had met for tea. The topic now seemed so fitting—the ephemerality of life, all life. That was one of the wonderful things about Professor Moody; when she asked what ephemerality meant, he didn't make her feel stupid, but he didn't tell her either. Professor Moody gave examples that would help her discover the meaning. He shared his knowledge and expanded hers. Adelina would miss spending time with him. Professor Moody had been so kind. Kindness was in short supply when it came to her life.

Fiona

Fiona felt robbed but couldn't say what had been taken. She only knew that with Professor Moody's passing, the space he had filled in her life would be empty again. The professor had brought her friendship, rapport, respect, anticipation, lightness. All things Fiona had distanced herself from without even realizing it.

How had she turned into such a lonely, cranky, just-past-middle-aged, single woman who drank too much wine and sat home on her days off watching TV for company? When Fiona was young, she had vowed never to become that kind of person. Now here she was, that kind of person. Exactly when had she stopped saying yes to life? *I can't tonight. I'm too tired. It's not my thing. Sounds exhausting. No can do, I have to work tomorrow.* Fiona had created excuses for everything. Now there was no need for excuses. Few invitations came her way.

Over the years many of her friends had moved out of Vancouver to places smaller, cheaper, simpler. A visit to see any of them was more than a one-day event. If any friends still lived in Vancouver, they were working, had families, or were too busy babysitting the grandkids. Plans to get together with them never seemed to materialize. As for her oldest friends, with little in common anymore, the conversations seemed to revolve around gastric reflux diagnoses, bad backs, or hearing about another one of their cruises. And so, like a lit candle, those friendships slowly burned down to nothing. But Professor Moody was different. In a short time, he had offered her so much when it came to friendship. But the thing he gave her the most was the desire to re-engage with her life.

There were many things Fiona knew for certain: There was no Prince Charming riding up on his trusty steed to take her away. There was no magical turning back of the clock. That if she didn't make changes, she'd keep existing in her current state of inertia, which was no way to live. When she caught up to Adelina at the bus stop after work, they rode together. They'd been doing that lately. The space between them held an understood silence. Professor Moody was dead, and they would both miss him.

Brice

First thing, Brice put his shamrock on the half-table by the window in his new room. Thankfully the table didn't jut out too much. There were only so many square feet to work with, and Brice needed to make use of each and every available spot. He looked around. *There really is such a thing as too much seafoam.* He was just thankful he got there before they painted the bathroom. Now fresco white, the bathroom walls were a close match with the newly mounted, raised, white toilet seat.

His eyes settled on what they had been trying to avoid, the elephant in the room—the used hospital bed OT Lisa had suggested he rent. Pride once again preventing him from practicality, he asked that it be placed to the left of the door so that when the door was open, it couldn't be seen from the hallway. "I don't need speculation from busybodies."

Brice pressed the call button for Tonia, the care aide. She made the bed and then lowered it as close to the floor as it would go. "It's easier for you to climb in and climb off at this level."

After she left, Brice lay down. The mattress sank slightly in the middle. He thought of Peter in hospice. The only thing less comfortable than his hospital bed, Peter had joked, would be one made of nails. Brice positioned himself first to the right and then left. Both times the sheets followed as he slid into the rock-hard, waterproof mattress. There was no way this bed would offer much in the way of comfort. Ever. Brice held onto the edges of the mattress with his eyes closed. He felt as if he were set adrift on an inflatable raft too far out from shore, all the while hanging on, praying he wouldn't drown in the wake of the rescue ship. Brice opened his eyes. No more hopes of travel—getting out of bed each day was going to be his grand adventure. Should the bed prove too much to deal with, Brice could always sleep on his La-Z-Boy. Diagonally placed, there'd been just enough room for it in the corner.

Staring at the recliner, Brice could see Peter. A curled-up cat, peacefully dozing, Brice would often watch him until Peter's pain became so uncontrollable that he had to move into hospice. Brice let go of the mattress. There was no rescue party coming to fetch him.

Adelina

Adelina looked out the bus window at the retreating image of Fiona heading home. She thought of Professor Moody. He had opened her up to the grand and the exciting—two words she had never used before when describing her life. Until he came along. It was comforting having Fiona to share in the loss she was feeling. Don was too busy worrying about himself to think of anyone else's troubles.

The sun was already starting to warm the day. The Farmer's Almanac in her bag promised a dry autumn with wonderful colour changes. She hoped it was right.

"I saw this at the checkout and got it for you," Don had said one rare day when he had done the grocery shopping. Even rarer was the Farmer's Almanac he handed her after getting his cigarettes out of the grocery bag. It touched her that Don, on one of his few good days, had done something nice. Usually, any extras were considered a big waste of money, except, of course, for his cigarettes and beer. His momentary act of thoughtfulness brought back memories of better times. Times when they had so much more in common than room and board. Adelina got off the bus and headed for the Skytrain.

Settling into a single window seat, Adelina spread the Farmer's Almanac on her lap. In this day of scientific certainty and circling satellites, it was reassuring that the Almanac was still there. A way to find small comfort in uncomfortable times. Adelina opened it up. "Bones thrown in the air," Don would sarcastically comment whenever he saw her reading it. *Well, I do read it, and I like to learn,* the small voice inside her said. Adelina had not heard that voice in some time. It scared her just a little to have "such ideas," as Don would call them. It pleased her too. Professor Moody would never have laughed at her for looking at the Almanac.

Adelina flipped through to the natural remedies section, but there was no natural remedy for what she needed—release. Adelina put the book back in her purse. Something inside her had shifted, but she couldn't say what that shift was. She got up from her seat—only one more bus to go.

Fiona

"Hey, Margaret." Fiona nudged her awake. "Any news on the new resident?"

Margaret lifted her face off the desk. Dazed, eyes half-opened, she looked up at Fiona and gave a wide yawn. It reminded Fiona of a webcam of a bear waking up from hibernation. "Oh, ah, the new resident. What...?"

"Yes, Margaret. The new resident. Remember, you were going to look at his report before first rounds?" Tonight was definitely a nap record. Fiona had gone off to check the emergency cart, a safety task done at the start of each shift. Margaret's job was to review the patient reports starting with the new resident. Fiona looked down at her watch, the hands glowing like a firefly in the dark. The time was 11:32 p.m. Taking into consideration Fiona's good-nights to the evening staff, removing and hanging up her coat, putting her lunch in the fridge, using the washroom, and checking the emergency cart, Fiona had been gone half-an-hour. She should have seen it coming when Margaret said her daughter had dropped off the kids. Runny noses and coughs, their daycare rightly sent them home. This turned into Margaret babysitting and not getting enough sleep.

"Oh, yes, sorry. I guess I nodded off. I was so busy with the grandkids. Fiona, here let me…"

"It's OK, Margaret. I have the report. We need to have information on him in case something happens." She liked to remind Margaret that this was a *we* situation.

Opening up the chart, Fiona felt like a teacher telling a story to her kindergarten class just before nap time to get them settled. Out loud she read, "Brice Sanderson, fifty-five." She put down the chart and looked at Margaret. This was not for effect. It was to check to see if Margaret was still awake.

"That's a bit young," Margaret answered, yawning again. Yes, it was just like kindergarten at nap time.

"How awful. He has ALS." One nurse to another, they shared a glance, an acknowledgement of what they both knew was coming for the poor man. Fiona scanned the report. "Grip is weak, gait unsteady. He uses a cane. Gets help with showering and dressing. This next one's flagged—he's on the list for a swallowing assessment. It looks like we need to be careful giving him anything by mouth. Oh, there must be bigger mobility issues— says he's also down for an electric wheelchair."

"So sad." Margaret finally looked awake.

"His GP referred him. He's been living in Azalea for the past six months. The doctor's report says Mr Sanderson's ALS is progressing quickly."

To Fiona, life was like a ride at the fair. Starting off slowly and then moving faster and faster. Up and down. Forward and backward. Unseen, the operator pulled the switch in total control. It sounded like this poor Mr Sanderson's ride was nearing its end.

A call bell interrupted the quiet. Fiona stopped reading. "Margaret, why don't you start looking through the lab work for the day, and I'll get this bell." Fiona put the report on the desk and picked up her flashlight.

Brice

Brice sat at the edge of his bed. Summer was turning into fall now. Would he see Christmas?

Brice, you gotta get off this negativity train. He slowly grabbed onto the recently installed overhead bar. The mattress was bare where the bottom sheet had slid away as he tried to raise himself up and off the bed. His pyjama bottoms had also made the slide and his rear end, now bare, rubbed against the exposed mattress. Out from under him came a noise which, if Brice were in public, he'd have had to either excuse himself for or blame on someone else. It was hard to remain positive when the universe kept sending messages that sounded like farts.

Finally able to stand, Brice struggled to get his bottoms up and then reached for his cane. His thoughts turned to pancakes. He visualized the rivulets of extra butter and maple syrup making trails down the stack of pancakes he planned on having. A Proustian moment, he could picture the butter and syrup collecting on his plate, ready for his forkful of pancake to soak up the tasty pool of maple butter goodness. Then, with a bite of fatty bacon applied to his fork, the morsel of perfection would be lifted gently and hopefully steadily to his mouth, the flavours mingling together—a taste straight from heaven.

But eating pancakes had turned into a daydream. The very act of swallowing was becoming more and more difficult. The fear of choking ever present, Brice now only ate soft foods. His thoughts returned to getting ready for the day. Everything took so much longer now; the second sitting for meals would be so much better for him. But joining the second sitting at the old folks' home was like winning the lotto. Old people, he was learning, didn't care anymore about being the early bird. Any worm-catching could happily be left for someone else. They'd rushed around most of their lives working and raising families. Now in their last years, they could sleep in and happily start their day later. Brice rang the bell for Tonia. Today was his bath day.

Washed and dressed, Brice looked down at the stain on his T-shirt. It was a one-season wear, but after hearing on the CBC about the link between fast fashion and overflowing landfills in Malaysia, Brice wanted to do his part. So he kept it. That's what Brice told people when they pointed to the stain and the frayed neckline. But his real reason for keeping the shirt was the panda on the front. Chomping down on his bamboo stick, the caption read, "I'm bamboozled." Which was perfect for the way Brice felt.

Brice stepped out into the hall, his right hand on the railing, his left holding his cane. He prayed another mobility-challenged resident wouldn't be coming the other way. Otherwise, it would be a stand-off at the O.K. Corral.

Finally, Brice reached his destination. He took a moment to look around at the walkers and canes attached to various residents heading into the dining room. Only a month ago, this had all been so new. Now here he was, part of the old folks' brigade, heading off to their latest mission: breakfast.

Adelina

If emptiness was nothing, Adelina wondered how a person could be so full of it. Coming home from work, Adelina thought of Don. The way he used to be. She needed *that* Don right now. Adelina stepped into their apartment. She could see Don sitting on the couch, staring at the muted TV screen. A sign. He was in one of his dangerous moods. A venomous snake that would lash out without warning.

Adelina called out, "It was a long night. I'm going straight to bed." Not bothering to look at her, Don just stared at the TV.

Lying in bed, Adelina's mind swirled with a marathon of thoughts, sleep her unattainable finish line. Four hours later, still awake, Adelina got up. Don had done nothing for days. No dishes. No laundry. No groceries. Adelina knew if Don was still sitting watching the TV on mute, it meant trouble. For her. Subterfuge her protective cape, Adelina slowly cracked open the door just enough to see out. Don was still sitting in his place in front of the silenced television. The only difference was the beer cans beside him. To her, Don resembled a statue set in stone. An artist's rendition of defeat. Adelina knew she had to get out of the apartment. Fast.

Quietly Adelina closed the door to the bedroom. Her breakfast would wait. She got dressed, then bundled up the dirty clothes. As she stepped into the hallway, Adelina called over her shoulder, "I'm going to the basement to do the laundry." Underground, underpaid, understaffed. How did her life become such a long list of unders? As she closed the door, Adelina looked back. Don, still blindly staring, never looked up once. She added undervalued to her list.

As Adelina stepped out of the elevator, she squinted, her eyes adjusting to the dim lighting (a building cost-saving measure). The damp coolness of the basement cut through her thin sweater. "Cost cutting, Adelina. We keep on just enough heat to keep the pipes from bursting," the building manager once told her. Did anyone plan to live their life in basements or, like her, did they somehow just end up there? Her thoughts turned to her childhood. Home had been a cramped apartment but she had loved it there; she had been safe and surrounded by love, unlike the cramped apartment she now lived in. Her dreams had been filled with Cinderella stories and female warrior adventures. Now her dreams had turned into nightmares as she went about her life, a captive in a dungeon.

Adelina laid her basket on the shared table. She rubbed her arms. The weight of a week's worth of dirty laundry made her arms feel as if they had been stretched on a rack by a Spanish inquisitor.

Are you or have you ever been a heretic?

No, your honour, I am innocent of all charges. Except for the act of being deceived by my husband.

How could Don be so thoughtless? Leaving all the work for

her again. But, if doing the laundry meant getting away from one of Don's moods, Adelina would gladly do it. The alternative would be pain. If only she could leave him. But leaving her husband was not included in her wedding vows. "Till death do us part." That was the contract Adelina naively promised before the eyes of God on her wedding day.

As usual, on Saturday morning, the laundry room was empty. People were off doing errands, sleeping in, or having brunch with friends. They weren't doing laundry, waiting for cycles to complete so they could get on to other chores. Not many ventured down into the dank laundry room unless a favourite pair of jeans was needed or company was arriving and there were no clean towels on offer.

For Adelina, the laundry room brought refuge. Being in a safe place with all its own familiar idiosyncrasies: The sound of coins disappearing as the slot closed. The rush of water echoing from the ceiling as it travelled through pipes from dishes done, teeth brushed, a toilet flushing. Metal on metal as she closed the dryer doors. The scrape of the lint screen pulled out and then pushed back in. The bang of a washing machine lid let go too soon. Footsteps of children above, running in the lobby, eager to get going on their Saturday morning. Down in the basement, to a fugitive on the run, these sounds meant there was life. Adelina closed her eyes and breathed in. The ever-present fragrance of laundry room soap over top of the musty smell of the underground filled her lungs. Adelina lifted the lids of three washing machines and started filling them with the various bundles from the laundry bag. Hot-water wash. Cold-water wash. Heavy. One day she would mix them all up just to see what happened. A rebel. The start of a laundry revolution. Until then, she'd keep doing what she was doing, an automaton of laundry automation.

Adelina took out her Farmer's Almanac hidden in the hamper. She felt like someone smuggling a treasure. For her, the treasure was reading in solitude. She'd take her time today. *Sorry I was so long. All the washers were in use.* God would forgive her these little lies. God had to know how tough it was living with a man whose only consideration was for himself. Behind her, the laundry room door banged open.

"Morning, Adelina. We've got to stop meeting like this." Helga gave her usual greeting.

"Morning, Helga. That's true, but where else would we go?" Adelina closed the Almanac.

Helga made her way over to the empty washers. "Guess I made it before June got here with all her loads."

On weekend mornings, if anyone else came to do laundry, it was mostly women like Adelina with nothing to do but household chores. They were the real weekend warriors. They sat—reading or texting, some nodding off, as their sheets tumbled dry—soothed by the dryer's rhythmic lullaby hum. Other times it was the irritation of the constant thump of drying shoes or the scraping of a coat's zipper against the drum.

"Adelina, can you watch my washer for me? I need to go upstairs," Helga, already at the laundry room door, asked her. "For the first time in a long time, we have company this weekend. My sister's visiting from Austria. We're having a late breakfast."

"Of course. I'm just sitting here. I know you'd do the same." Both of them knew Adelina would never ask such a favour. There were never any visitors at Adelina's.

Sitting there reading, warmed by the dryer's exhaust, Adelina felt anger. Never did Don ever consider that maybe she wanted to have some quiet time. That it should be him doing the groceries and laundry, or meeting up with one of his few remaining friends for coffee. A small gift, some private time alone, would give her time to drink tea and read a book. Maybe watch a TV show that she liked. If she could remember what she liked. It would be good for Don to get out. Why was it always her, escaping?

Her wash done and folded and Helga back, Adelina headed upstairs. Don was still looking at the TV, drinking beer. She counted the crushed cans. If this drinking kept up, the monster would show itself. Beer was the Dr Jekyll potion of choice.

"I'm off to get something for dinner. Maybe stop by church for mass. Is there anything we need?" she asked, searching her purse for money.

"Peanut butter."

It wasn't that Don was good for nothing—because he was good at something: he was good at costing her, costing her time and money and effort. The ledger balance weighed heavily on her side. It was against God's word, but sometimes Adelina found herself fantasizing about life without him. *I'm new to mushroom gathering, officer. I must have mixed up the harmful and the safe. Would they even do an autopsy?* The morgues were so busy with the overdose crisis. When one of the parishioners' sons passed, they had no room in the morgue for him. He was sent, on ice like a fish at the market, to someplace outside of Vancouver. Would the coroner even waste time on an out-of-shape drunk? Other women dreamed of trips to Europe; some dreamt of handsome, rich men driving them off to mountain getaways, taking them away from the lives they lived. Adelina dreamt the dream of the abused. Fright. Flight. Fight. Don out of her life was becoming her fantasy. It almost didn't matter how he left. Just that he would be gone. How had it come to this—her thinking about something so against one of God's commandments?

Fiona

I could be on the moon looking for...? What did they look for on the moon anyway? Water? Rocks? The man in the...? Fiona did a sweep with her flashlight, right to left, left to right, down the dimly lit hall. She walked by the nook in the Paris-themed bistro where she, Professor Moody, and Adelina used to meet up. Fiona sat at their table and turned off her flashlight. The light over the kitchen sink gave off just enough light to see. Had it really only been three weeks since he died?

Professor Moody hadn't wanted any fuss. A man of science, he chose to be cremated and have his ashes spread. But Fiona believed in funerals, in celebrations of life. Recognition for a life lived was important. People who said they didn't want any kind of service didn't understand. It wasn't for them; they were gone. It was to give those left behind an act three of the tragedy.

"Such a good-looking man. Couldn't they find a photo with a smile?" Margaret complained when they had looked at his online obit. If anything, Margaret knew a good obituary when she saw one. When not looking at Facebook, Margaret scanned the obituaries section of her online *Vancouver Sun*. "I'm always looking for ideas."

Stretching her legs out straight to ease the ache in her lower back, Fiona looked around. The tables were covered in yellow and blue tablecloths. Daytime, should anyone want the full French feel, they stocked the cupboards with Costco croissants, madeleines, and French roast coffee. By night, when the three of them had met up for their chats, all that was left of the croissants and cookies were the crumbs waiting for Adelina and her broom.

Fiona was glad at least that Calla Lily Tower was recognizing the professor's death with a tea. They did that for the residents who died—let those assembled see the dearly departed as a whole person from birth to grave. Fiona heard from Margaret that a couple of his nephews were coming all the way from Nova Scotia to represent the family. The rest of his immediate family couldn't come. They were elderly and a long trip from the Maritimes was no longer possible. Of course, Fiona would be there. She felt a deep need to share her loss with others. Lessen it by spreading it around, the last bit of jam in the jar.

Was that a scream? Fiona hurried down the hall following the voice. She stopped at the professor's old door. The yelling was coming from inside.

"Mr Sanderson, it's the nurse. I'm coming in." Fiona took a deep breath to ready herself. With a scream, you never knew what you'd find. Someone in a medical crisis, or laying on the floor after a fall, or being sick in a wastebasket, or waking from a nightmare. Opening the door, Fiona stepped into the room. What a way to meet the new resident.

Brice

"Hi sis, how are you?" Brice leaned into his computer.

"Good, thanks. I'm sorry I haven't come to see you yet. I plan on getting out there."

"To remind you, I do have ALS. If you wait long enough, you can change my diaper."

"Now, Brice, don't be like that. I'm sitting behind a mountain of files. The temp replacing our usual receptionist had a sweet deal, I'll tell you. The bare minimum would be an exaggeration. Then there's Sam. You know he hates flying."

"How does he get to Florida every year?"

"That's different. So you had a fall? How did that happen?"

"Like most falls. I tripped. Unfortunately, over my own feet."

"Was it because of the ALS? Is it progressing?"

"Thanks sis, for not saying my ALS. It isn't mine. I don't want it."

"I know Brice. I know."

"It amazes me how a person can end up owning something they didn't want in the first place."

"People don't mean to reduce you to a disease. Not on purpose. It's just that maybe they can't find the words for what they want to say." Marcia sounded like she was searching for the words herself.

"I keep thinking of Uncle Jim," Brice whispered into the computer.

"I think of him too. We were so little the last time we saw him. That day was horrible. I was so frightened. When Mom and Dad said we were going home and didn't have to go back, I was so happy. Sometimes I wonder how poor Uncle Jim felt about it."

"Funny, we've never talked about that day. I didn't realize you felt that way. I did too." Brice remembered Marcia as they headed home, quiet and pale, leaning against the corner of the back seat of the car. Maybe that was why Marcia hadn't been to visit him. She was scared, not only for him but for herself.

Brice changed the subject. "A nurse named Fiona helped me. I was so lucky she heard me calling. She had this big, old, badass flashlight. Honestly, when I saw her light, I thought I was headed for the tunnel and there was no coming back. When she checked me over, I scored fourteen out of fifteen on the how's-the-patient-doing scale—a better grade than I ever got at school. I lost one point for thinking she was God. Got to say, I wasn't disappointed that God was female."

"Don't be sacrilegious."

"I'm joking. I lost a point because of my motor skills. But that wasn't from the fall." Brice was not in the mood for this. His bum still hurt, and his right hand did too. His head wasn't feeling all that great either. He and Marcia travelled their lives down such different roads. It sometimes seemed like he needed a map to find her.

"Did you go to hospital?"

"I refused."

"What if you're hurt?"

"Nurse Fiona checked on me every hour and the doctor-on-call came later that morning and gave me the once over."

"I am so glad you're in a place that can take care of you. How's the food? I hear so many homes have poor-quality food."

Somehow their conversations always came down to the banal. "Yes, I'm eating. I don't need help yet if that is what you are getting at."

"Now, Brice, be careful. You've got Mom's gene for weight gain."

"Is there a beauty contest at the funeral home I need to be on the watch for?"

"Think of your pallbearers." Marcia laughed.

It was nice to see her joking. "Oh, the Sanderson humour's coming out now, is it? Just for that, I'm making you a pallbearer. Truth is, I'm losing weight and not in a good way. I have difficulty swallowing. I'm on a soft food diet which isn't all that enticing. I'm also losing muscle mass."

Marcia's phone rang. "I'm so sorry. I have to answer that. It's probably Jennifer; she's having trouble finding an invoice we need to process. I'll call back later."

Staring at the laptop screen, it occurred to Brice that even though they had been joking around, on some level, he and Marcia had been discussing his death.

Adelina

Wednesday was railing night. Adelina took the disinfectant-soaked rag in her gloved hand and cupped it around the rail. With a wide stance, she rhythmically moved it along the railing. She pictured herself in a small boat, rowing in time with the gently moving water—the sun, warm on her back; the breeze, a gentle tickle on her face. Maybe one day she would take a cruise and head off somewhere warm, away to a place where she might feel happy.

As she reached the door to Professor Moody's old room, her memories of him tripped her up. Adelina stopped. Railing night was how she had first met Professor Moody—bent over and wiping down the underside of the banister when he came out of his room and nearly bumped into her.

Adelina remembered how she'd kept apologizing— "I'm sorry, sir. I didn't mean to startle you"—her head bowed in deference as she spoke. Adelina was only a cleaner; this man was someone who paid her salary. The balance of power was tipped to his side. Her side of the scale was hanging up in the air, waiting for the drop.

Instead, he laughed. "I'm the one who came barreling out of my room, not looking where I was going. I didn't expect anyone to be so intent on cleaning. Thank you for being so thorough in your duties. Please know it's appreciated. Why don't you join me for a cup of tea? I have some chocolate biscuits. Oh, and please excuse me. I'm Michael Moody." The professor had offered his hand.

"Yes, Professor Moody. I see it on your door. I'm Adelina." Respect for age and education made Adelina use his full title. "It is time for my break. Do you think they would get upset if I had tea with you?"

"I'm not sure whom you mean by they, but as a paying resident, I get to invite whomever I want to invite. I'm inviting you." That was how their friendship had started.

Always a night owl, Professor Moody would read and study into the wee hours. Most nights he'd head to the kitchenette before bed to have herbal tea and biscuits. He had told her that first night, pouring Adelina a cup of raspberry tea, "There are plenty of people here I can talk to, but half of them are waiting for death to claim them and the other half just want to talk about their various aches, pains, and upcoming surgeries."

Adelina had to agree—these were not the most interesting conversations for an educated man trying to stimulate his brain. It made her proud—a feeling she was not always in touch with—that she, Adelina, was considered to offer stimulating conversation and that Professor Moody wanted to spend time with her. There were so few people left in her life that did. Don had seen to that. Slowly he'd separated her from her family and friends. Now the only contact she had with most of her friends was an occasional phone call or Christmas card.

Passing by what only a few days ago had been his room, Adelina looked up at the closed door. The sign on it said Mr Brice Sanderson. How fast some things could change.

Fiona

An endless stream of cars filled the parking lot and crowded the street in front of Calla Lily Tower. It was a good thing Waterview was using their large conference room for Professor Moody's celebration of life. Fiona met up with Adelina outside the front door.

"I almost didn't recognize you, Fiona. You look so different out of your uniform." Adelina said shyly.

"You too, Adelina." Fiona looked around at the growing crowd. "Isn't the turnout wonderful? I had no idea Professor Moody knew this many people. I'm crying already, and we haven't gotten through the door yet."

Fiona watched Adelina take a small engraved box from her purse and hold it up. "I brought tissues." The engraving looked like some kind of saint with a halo.

"Is my mascara smudged?" Fiona pulled a tissue from the box then dabbed under her eyes. "My mother would be so proud of me. She used to shudder when I left the house undone, as she put it. I can just hear her, 'Put on some make-up Fiona; there may be a few unattached men.'" Fiona saw Adelina's face registering shock. "I'm joking, Adelina. It's just that I rarely get out anymore. It's nice to wear make-up now and again. Get dressed in something other than my baggy, blue, polyester uniform." Fiona looked around. "Do you recognize anyone?" Adelina shook her head. "Me neither. I'm really bad at mingling. I've never been good at making small talk."

"Neither have I," admitted Adelina.

Fiona thought she saw a look of apprehension as Adelina watched the two lines forming to enter. "At things like these I stand close to an exit. I call it my 'get out of Dodge' plan. Just in case I get stuck with someone who wants to tell me their life story. Anyone interesting or exciting never seems to talk to me for very long." Fiona laughed.

"The only crowd I am in is at St Thomas Aquinas mass," Adelina said. "I really don't know as many people there as I used to. Like so many churches, we've become a smaller, older congregation. But at Sunday morning mass, the days when I'm not working, my old church friends and I visit for a bit after the service. Otherwise, I really only talk to Don, coworkers, and a few people from the apartment building."

"Why don't we be each other's wingwomen?" Fiona smiled. "I really don't want to be alone either."

An attendant handed Fiona and Adelina a memorial card.

"Look Adelina, it says here Professor Moody's two nephews from Nova Scotia are speaking." Fiona could see Margaret waving them over. With that they joined Margaret in line and, together, they headed into the building.

Brice

Looking out the window of the Calla Lily Tower lobby, Brice could see the crowd of people gathering at the entranceway. Waterview was having a memorial for the man whose room he had taken. By the looks of the number of people attending, the man must have been loved and respected. It made Brice wonder what his celebration would be like, or even if there'd be one. One thing for certain, Brice knew his death wouldn't be unexpected.

Adelina

Adelina watched the crowd as they headed home. She sent up a prayer of thanks to God. It was good to be part of this team of people, caring for the elderly and infirm. They all had a purpose no matter how big or how small their roles. Adelina wasn't surprised one bit to learn how much Professor Moody had been loved. His nephews' eulogy told of his encouragement and direction—how they had both become teachers because of him.

Professor Moody's fellow professors had taken to the podium and spoken of his milestones and achievements. Each speaker told of his love of family, students, and friends. Adelina regretted not going to the front and speaking when the group was asked to share some sentiment or story. Such a large crowd of learned people intimidated her. But she did gather the courage to tell his nephews how much their uncle had meant to her. In turn, they let her know how much Adelina had meant to the Professor.

"We know you didn't know Uncle all that long, but when we called, he often spoke of you to us." His nephew Jordan took her hand. "We were so happy Uncle Michael met someone he felt he could talk to. Most of his friends are older now and getting around isn't that easy for them."

Someone the Professor could talk to? Her? If a spirit lifting could be measured, they'd have seen Adelina's stretched to the sky.

Fiona and Adelina headed to the cloakroom. "Want to try that pub we always see from the bus?" Fiona whispered to Adelina. "It's close by. I don't know how you fared at the buffet table, but all I got was two water crackers and the last of the cheese spread. I felt like Oliver Twist looking at his bowl of gruel." Fiona batted her eyes.

"I really should head home—Don's expecting me."

"We never go out! One hour. A glass of wine and some chicken wings. I only use it for emergencies, but, hey, call him on my cell." Fiona dug into her purse and held the flip phone out for Adelina.

"You can go, but make damn sure you come back right afterward," Don told her.

Adelina hadn't gone out with a friend since she and Joni went to their office Christmas dinner. "OK, I guess an hour won't hurt." But when Adelina got home, it hurt. It hurt badly.

Fiona

"Hello Brice." Fiona said, looking down at Brice as he lay on the floor. Adelina followed in behind her and stood by the door. "We've got to stop meeting like this. Fortunately, Adelina here heard you calling and came and got me. Are you hurting anywhere? Does anything feel broken?"

"Just my pride," Brice answered.

"Well, at least you didn't lose your sense of humour." Stepping around him Fiona's eyes searched the floor. "Do you remember hitting your head?"

"I don't know."

"Do you know if you lost consciousness?" Fiona asked, kneeling beside him.

"I don't think so." Brice sounded unsure. "One minute I was thinking about getting a drink of water from the bathroom. The next minute I was admiring the ceiling. Not that it's the Sistine Chapel or anything, but the dim lighting from the hall casts some interesting shadows. Just in case you ever have nothing to do on your break."

Taking out her pen-light, Fiona checked his eyes. His pupils looked equal and reactive. Then she tested his muscle strength.

There were no changes that she could discern from the night before, when he had last fallen. "Brice, I'm going to call an ambulance. We need you to get seen at the hospital. For now, I need you to stay still in case you have an injury I can't see."

"Not the hospital. Please."

Fiona knew people were afraid of going to the hospital. It was as if they thought they wouldn't come home. Sadly, sometimes they were right. "I know this is hard for you. Most likely nothing is wrong, but I worry you might have a concussion. Since this is your second fall in as many days, there could be something brewing. The only way we can know for sure is to have them take a better look."

"Can't it just be that I'll have a bruise to match the one I already have?" Brice said, the tears falling from his eyes.

Fiona leaned over and took a tissue from the box on his over-bed table. Gently, she wiped his eyes. "I realize it's late, but, Brice, can I call someone to meet you at the hospital?" Fiona knew from his chart that his next of kin was his sister, in Ontario.

"No." Brice turned his face toward the wall.

Fiona got up off the floor. "Adelina, can you please stay by Brice and help remind him not to move?"

As she headed to the nursing station to call an ambulance, Fiona wondered, with billions of people in the world, how could so many, her included, be so alone.

Brice

Brice tried lifting his head from the floor, but Adelina quietly reminded him that he needed to stay still. "Just until they get you to hospital." He watched as she tucked the blanket around his shoulders.

"At least this time I didn't go face first." He winced. He was wet from pissing his diaper, embarrassed, and hurt from his fall. But more than anything, Brice was scared. Life was abandoning him.

Brice thought about the night two days before when nurse Fiona had helped him, how he'd held onto her, not wanting to be left while she got help to get him back to bed. The emotion he felt at that moment was as deep as the emotion he felt on his first day of school as he clung onto his mother, begging her not to leave him behind. Brice remembered his mother pulling his little hands off her to get free of his grip. Even now, Brice could feel the cold of the chain link on his face and the wet of his tears as he leaned on the fence, watching his mother walk away from him. That day Brice learned the hard truth of life. Ultimately, each of us are on our own. Now here he was, back on the floor, a beached whale waiting for the tide to take him back to the sea.

What time is it anyway? He wasn't able to see the clock. He could ask Adelina, but what did it matter, really? It was always funny to him how when you were enjoying things, time passed by in a nanosecond. Now, laying on the floor waiting, time became a slow-moving turtle.

What was left for him? All the things he couldn't do. No trip to France. No leisurely drive across Canada taking in the sights. No Mardi Gras. No more breathing easily. No more not wearing a diaper.

He started to sob. "I'm going to die in this nursing home, Adelina. Maybe even right now on this floor." He sobbed harder as Adelina tried to comfort him. But there was no comfort to be had.

Adelina

"I've never been so afraid," Brice told her as they sat waiting for Fiona to return with the news of the ambulance. "I've got ALS. That's why I keep falling," he confided in a scratchy whisper. "It's getting worse every day. I'm scared, Adelina. I feel like a fox caught in a trap. Please don't leave me."

As he told her this, Adelina looked down at his bruised, frightened face. She had no idea what ALS meant. All Adelina knew as she sat there, holding his hand, was that it didn't sound good. Not good at all. They say no one really knows what another person is going through, but in the stillness of the night, Adelina thought she knew. She too had those same soul-deep feelings of utter loneliness.

Fiona

When Fiona had taken this job, she hadn't counted on how much the patients would mean to her. And even though it had been such a short time working at Calla Lily Tower, the residents had become like family. Even Margaret was like an annoying cousin you were made to visit and then were surprised you actually wanted to see again after you left.

Making her way to the nursing station, she ran through the list of what she had to do:

- *Ask Margaret to call the ambulance*
- *Get Brice's chart together and copy the necessary documents for the paramedic*
- *Go back and stay with Brice until the ambulance comes*
- *Remain professional and don't cry at the unfairness of it all*

Brice

As he made his way over to his La-Z-Boy, Brice leaned heavily on the walker the occupational therapist at the hospital had advised. He looked like a man of eighty. He felt like a man of ninety. Brice sat down and maneuvered his wheeled, overbed table closer using the handle of his cane. Now that he was using a walker, he used the cane for such purposes as bringing things closer, pushing things away, and shutting the door to his room. To make life easier, he kept his laptop open on the overbed table. His life was becoming more modified with each passing week.

Slowly Brice typed MAID into the browser. There it was, right after cleaning services. Brice clicked on the medical assistance in dying link and started reading. There were two options. Both needed a doctor or a nurse practitioner and their signature. *Probably to prevent your family from offing before you're ready to go.* Brice scrolled down.

You could be given a substance that caused death, such as an injection. This was known as clinician-administered medical assistance in dying, previously known as voluntary euthanasia. But was it ever really voluntary? No one just volunteers to die if they don't have to. The second option was to be provided with a drug the person could take themselves, also known as self-administered medical assistance in dying, previously known as medically-assisted suicide or assisted suicide. Brice looked at both choices. *By the time I get this in motion, I'll hardly be able to swallow a sip of tea without choking, let alone swallow pills.* He'd go with the clinician-assisted. Brice scrolled down further to a death and dying website. He clicked onto the blog.

By the looks of it, everyone chatting on the site was happy with their decision to end their lives with MAID (not that anyone could ask them how it went once it was done). The other entries were from family and friends who had attended a death. Brice stopped reading. He hadn't thought about inviting people. Were there invitation cards for such a thing? Embossed with your choice of gold or silver? *Please join me in my upcoming going away party?* Did you send out a mass email? A group text? Post a status update on Facebook? Maybe make a TikTok video with Freddy Mercury singing, "Another One Bites the Dust."

Who would he invite anyway? He'd barely kept in touch with friends after Peter died; it might be awkward inviting someone to your death when you haven't seen them in a while. And what if nobody came? It'd be just like his ninth birthday party. Brice's mother had invited the entire class and only six out of twenty-nine kids showed. Could Brice face such humiliation again? On his deathbed no less? He'd have to get someone to send out a post-death Trump inauguration brag. *Biggest crowd ever in the history of MAID. No one's seen anything like it. It was HUGE!*

Brice continued reading. A few of the posts said they were shocked when they first learned that their loved one wanted MAID, but came to accept it when they saw how their loved one was suffering. Another person who had attended their spouse's MAID wrote about not wanting moral debates—they only shared the experience with people who agreed with their partner's decision. Someone else said they made peace with the fact their loved one wanted MAID even while they were in turmoil because they were losing their loved one (but weren't they going to lose their loved one sooner or later?). Another entry said the person didn't want any hoopla—just the shot.

All in all, the comments were positive for those able to die at home or in the facility where they lived. It wasn't so positive if the person had to go somewhere else to have their final wishes carried out, because not all facilities were equipped to support or agreed with MAID. Brice prayed Waterview did.

He scrolled to the 'how-to' portion of the site. There was a request form to download and fill in. *Even when you want to die there's a form.* Brice would need to find two witnesses to sign it, no family. When completed, his form went to an assessment team. From there two health care providers—either physicians or nurse practitioners, or one of each, would assess whether or not Brice was eligible for MAID. One of those two providers assessing his request would be the one performing his MAID.

Next step, he'd have an initial meeting with the provider via Skype, Facetime, or a phone call. If the situation warranted, there might be an in-person meeting. After that there would be a reflective period of ten days before Brice could have his MAID. *I have to wait ten days? Even Amazon delivers in less than 5!* A registered nurse would also accompany the provider to insert the intravenous. The IV was for access so the medications could be administered. If Brice needed help arranging things, there was a clinical coordinator that would help with logistics like contacting the funeral home to take away the body. *Didn't even think about what to do with my body.* Brice read further. If you changed your mind, you could say no at any time.

Now how to tell Marcia. Or, how not to tell her. Should he invite her? Would she come? She hadn't bothered to come out yet to see him. Maybe he should let her think he died of natural causes? Brice pushed away his table with his cane.

All he wanted was to get MAID. Not spend precious time doing research, sending off invites, booking a room, and picking an outfit. He just wanted to go peacefully, and soon. Hopefully, the front office at Waterview could help him. They must have something in place for such requests. Surely not everyone in Calla Lily Tower slipped away in their sleep or died after a fall. Brice picked up the phone and asked for Theresa, the Calla Lily Manager.

Adelina

Finally, it was break time. Her exhaustion to the bone, every muscle ached. She had had little sleep and Holly had not shown up again. There was no one to replace her. More and more there seemed to never be any replacement. Taking her mop out of the pail of blackened water, Adelina recalled God's words: "Blessed is the man who remains steadfast under trial." She squeezed the mop dry and put it back in her cart.

Needing time on her own, she headed to the bistro. And even though Holly being off made extra work for her, Adelina felt empathy. Holly's two sons were growing into troubled youths. She often came home to overturned beer cans and spilled marijuana on the living room table—her sons too stoned to get up and go to school. Holly must have taken time off to watch them. This worried Adelina. The last time Holly called in sick, the manager put her on notice. She'd been told that any more absences wouldn't be tolerated—that they'd put her on suspension. Why was it, Adelina wondered, some people lived under storm clouds while others had gentle breezes at their backs?

As she sat drinking a cup of tea at the table she and the professor used to share, she thought about that morning, when she got home from work. Don had been at the door waiting—on another one of his rampages. As he towered over her shouting about how bad his life was, how he should have left years ago, how she didn't care, it felt as if Adelina was an observer looking down at them both. For the first time, she didn't try and appease him or worry about why he felt the way he did or what she could do to help him. Neither did she look for an escape route. Adelina just stood there, thinking about how she hated Don's foul breath smelling of stale beer, and his greasy, unwashed hair. How angry she was he couldn't be bothered to change his clothes for days even though every morning she left a clean shirt and pants out for him. How fed-up she was with his abuse. How drained she was by the very sight of him. Thinking of what she'd been through that morning, the tears poured from her eyes like a burst pipe.

Don was becoming more and more crazed. As he stood shouting, she had felt fear like never before. But from somewhere deep within herself, Adelina understood that in that fear, there could be power. That morning, she came to the realization she could not fix him. He was like a tornado touching down, ripping through, tearing her spirit into pieces, and there was nothing she could do to stop it. But what Adelina could do, what she knew she had to do, was take control of the aftermath.

Her break over, Adelina got up to wash and dry her cup before putting it away. Then, as she headed through the doorway of the bistro back to work, she knew within her very being what was going to happen. She was going to find a way to be free.

Fiona

Fiona badly wanted to talk to Adelina at break, but there had been no chance to meet up—she'd been busy helping Margaret send Mr Williams to hospital. The poor man didn't have long. Now, off late from work, standing alone at the bus stop waiting to go home, it was as if the cool morning breeze was sweeping up the shock Fiona was feeling.

She had found Brice awake when she checked on him in the early hours. Fiona had turned the light on low and gone into his room. That was when he had asked her. He wanted her to be present at his MAID.

That alone was hard enough for Fiona to deal with. What was harder were her words to him—they had flowed out of Fiona in a stream of selfishness. Her shame at what she had said to him was a black cloud making her mood dark. But his request seemed to come out of nowhere. Her shock at what he asked of her made Fiona feel like she'd waded into the ocean, suddenly finding the drop off point. Listening to him, she felt like she was going under, gasping for air, her feet searching for firmer footing.

And even though she heard his request, she hadn't truly listened. What Fiona had done instead was to throw what she saw as options at Brice, like a woman flinging her philandering husband's clothes onto the street. "They're working on so many new advances with ALS. Health Canada's being pressured to approve investigational medications sooner. There are alternative medications for pain control. Marijuana, for instance. Palliative care is better than ever." Fiona kept going. "I know living with ALS is hard. But medical assistance in dying? How can you even think such a thing! You're not ready."

Then, her tirade finished, Fiona had looked down at Brice lying in his bed. She'd seen him as he was, not how she wanted him to be. Her eyes were opened to his truth, not hers. The head of his bed was now always raised to help him breathe. His breaths were short and rapid, artillery gunfire attempts to get air. From the nursing report, Fiona knew he was being assessed for a CPAP machine to help him breathe at night. As she stood over him, watching him labour for each breath, she knew it was more than likely he'd need to wear the CPAP during the day as well. She watched as he fought to keep his eyelids, half-open blinds, from closing. He looked so very tired.

Fiona knew that, with a debilitating illness, lifting your weakened body in and out of bed, or up and down out of a chair, or on and off the toilet, could do that to you. Eating, talking, laughing, crying, trying to breathe, could do that to you. Who was she to tell Brice he wasn't ready? He was the one living with ALS, not her. He was the one dying of ALS not her. A diagnosis of a terminal illness was like dangling from a hangman's rope while the noose took its time. Sometimes it might be wiser to choose the firing squad.

"Forgive me, Brice," she had told him. "This isn't my journey. It's yours."

Now, waiting for the bus, Fiona wondered why in the hell she'd said "journey." Everything these days, from going to the dentist to having cancer to buying a pair of shoes, was now under the personal journey umbrella. Being on a "journey" sounded like you were going off to explore the Amazon, or see the pyramids, or walk the Camino. What Brice was doing was facing his mortality—morally, emotionally, physically. Fiona was only a bystander. Brice didn't need a sermon from her or anyone else telling him about taking a journey. And even though they had met only a short while ago, she didn't want to see him go. It was hard losing someone you cared for.

She thought back to when he had said to her, his voice slurred, "I've been so very blessed these last few weeks living at Water-view. Getting help. Meeting you and Adelina. I've had many good rides around planet earth. It's time for me to get off and see what else is out there waiting for me. I don't want to die, but I'm going to. For me, MAID is the best option. I'll be fine. I get to be with Peter."

The bus pulled up and Fiona got on. As the bus drove into the traffic, she stared out the window at the unfolding day. Everywhere there were people, coloured tacks being moved around on a map by some unseen hand. Some were heading off to work; mothers, their children lagging behind, being dragged off to school; young men in suits, bent down to pick up after their dogs; delivery drivers skirted through traffic. And she was going home to bed. Life went on.

If she were in Brice's place, she wouldn't hesitate to ask for MAID. She'd seen enough suffering and pain to know the release that would be offered with medical assistance in dying. But now, being asked to attend a friend's planned death, her moral compass was off kilter. But no way would she leave Brice without a send-off. She'd be there to catch his streamer and hold onto it until Brice sailed away and it broke and she was left behind on shore.

Fiona didn't know the rules around attending the MAID of a friend who was a resident where she worked. When she got home, she'd call the nursing college to make sure her being there wouldn't be a conflict. Fiona only hoped that Brice was choosing to end his life for the right reasons and not because of finances or because he didn't want to be a burden. That he was choosing death because life was no longer palatable. Wasn't that the right reason?

She got off the bus at her street.

All the rules had changed, which could be disconcerting if you didn't keep up. But it was good too. Pot was legal. Dying your hair neon green wasn't laughable. No one pointed to your unmatched socks like you had committed a mortal crime. There was no more being left to suffer and die a slow, painful, humiliating death if you didn't want to.

Brice

As he sat waiting for Marcia to join the Skype call, Brice tested his voice. "Me, me, me, me." *Even Donald Duck would be an improvement.* With all of his bruises he looked like an eggplant past its due date. Why couldn't Marcia just go with a telephone call?

Suddenly Marcia's face peered out at him. "Brice, is that you?"

"I look so bad you don't recognize me?"

"No one looks good on a computer. What's the matter?" Marcia's look was one of concern.

The matter? For fuck's sake, I'm going to die. That's what's the matter. "Can I ask what you think might be the matter?" Brice waited.

"Brice, please. Is this going to be one of those arguments where we go round and round like a dog chasing its tail?"

"How could you not know, Marcia?"

Outside his window, the clouds drifted, getting ready to rain, and the bright morning was now blocked by shadow. Brice got it. Marcia didn't need to look out at the world for answers or understanding or awareness. Her faith was her anchor. Brice's was what? Peter? But Peter had been dead for six years now. There was no point continuing in a bitter argument in what he knew most likely would be one of their last conversations.

Everyone has a closet of their own they hide in at some time or another. Marcia's was her comfortable, settled life. Hadn't he hidden for years in his own closet, pretending to be straight? Brice had no desire to shatter her world with his decision. No matter their differences, he loved his sister. There was no one else left on this earth Brice shared as much with—DNA, parents, childhood, his coming out.

When he had decided to come out, Brice told her first, hoping she would be his ally. She had been too. In the way that only Marcia could. "Mom, Dad, I know being gay isn't what you wanted for your children and it goes against our religious beliefs. But Brice is Brice and that Brice is gay, so we may as well accept it." And with heavy hearts they had accepted it. They even attended his and Peter's wedding vows, but declined the invitation to the reception.

At the time, seeing how hurt Brice had been, Peter had joked, "Too many gays?" But his family supported his marriage in their own way. Now, with his death approaching, Brice owed it to his sister to be as open with her as he had been all those years ago. Brice would accept whatever Marcia decided about his plan to use MAID. Be there, don't be there—he needed to leave this earth on loving terms, his terms.

"Marcia, I've decided to go ahead with medical assistance in dying. I'd like it if you could be with me. I understand if you can't."

Adelina

Getting up to go to get ready for work, Adelina thought back to what Brice had asked her that morning. She had felt unequipped to help him.

"My life is heading down the pooper, Adelina. My disease is progressing fast." She'd sat beside Brice's bed, her right hand holding his. "I'm going to die." Adelina could see his breathing was shallow and quick. "Even if they came out with a cure today, the damage done can never be fixed."

Adelina watched as Brice stopped to catch his breath before continuing with his laundry list of losses, his voice a whisper, his words slurred. "My muscles are weak. I've had those two bad falls. The ER doctor said I need to use my wheelchair all the time now. I'm down to liquids and after that I'll need a tube. I'm getting assessed for a breathing machine. When I eventually lose my voice, there's a machine for that too. I'll get to sound like a robot from an old Star Trek episode." Brice stopped again. Adelina watched as his chest rose and fell quickly. "I'll be like that clunker car we've all owned at some time or other. You keep working on it, but it can never run like new."

Adelina squeezed his hand. "Why are you telling me all of this,

Brice? I'm only a cleaner. Let me pray for you."

"I know we hardly know each other. But the other night when you helped me after my fall, and now these past few days, you coming to see me... I've felt a bond between us. I feel like you understand me. Like you care. Maybe your faith makes me trust you. Or maybe I'm just desperate. I don't really know."

No one had ever spoken to Adelina like this before. It was all so raw.

"I'm in a battle, Adelina. ALS will be the victor. I've decided I don't want to continue like this. I don't know how you feel about it, but I've chosen medical assistance in dying. Would you honour me by being present at my MAID? You don't have to do anything, just be with me."

Adelina had pulled her hand away from his. Suicide was not something she could condone. And yet, she didn't want to be unkind. Looking down at him, she saw his fear. How could she not help him? "Before I answer, I need to ask God."

"OK, Adelina, but please ask him to hurry." Brice laughed. All she could do was pretend to smile.

Fiona

Sitting at their favourite spot in the bistro, Fiona and Adelina sipped their tea. They needed to talk about Brice's request that they be there for his MAID; a difficult topic for the both of them. They were avoiding it.

"Fiona, what happened to Mrs Ferguson after you sent her to hospital last night?"

"I got the call just before I left work. She died shortly before getting to the emergency department. I feel so bad. She was all alone in the back of the ambulance." Fiona looked over at Adelina. Her face looked as if she'd been thrown into cold water. "There was no one here that could accompany her, and her family didn't answer when I called." Fiona felt like she was explaining her own failings, adding, "The paramedic seemed like a really nice man. I watched him. His words were very kind."

Fiona's explanation wasn't only for Adelina's benefit. She was trying to convince herself that Mrs Ferguson had been properly cared for. "From what I can gather, her family didn't visit very often. It was as if she was something put away in a cupboard and then forgotten about."

"Does that happen often? Families not visiting?"

"More than you want to know, Adelina. We get reports from the day shift. They let us know if a resident has been stood up for a day out or left alone on the holidays. If we find someone awake on our rounds after such an upset, we make sure to take a few minutes to sit with them and try to get them to settle, but they aren't stupid—they know they've been forgotten." Fiona always found this difficult—comforting those left behind.

"I had no idea such things happened. I sometimes see people up during the night. That's how I got to know Professor Moody. We're told not to say anything but hello, or ask if they need us to get the nurse. But sometimes, if they want, I take time to talk to them."

"It's often those small moments that mean the most to the person on the receiving end." Fiona thought about how often she felt humbled by the thanks she got for even just peeking in to see how someone was doing.

"Those small moments are like when God talked about the mustard seed."

"The mustard seed?" At first, when Adelina talked this way, Fiona thought she was preaching or trying to recruit her to go to church. Until she realized Adelina's beliefs were as much a part of her as her voice, her face, her hands.

Adelina closed her eyes and recited, "Which indeed is the least of all seeds, but when it is grown, it is the greatest among herbs and becometh a tree, so that the birds of the air come and lodge in the branches thereof."

"Adelina, you couldn't find a better verse. When I do find a resident who has been left behind, I try and remember that most families are there visiting every week and more. I also remember that not every family is happy. Some relatives might be more than justi-fied in not visiting. And there are those residents who have simply outlived everyone. Many at Calla Lily are over eighty. Even if their family and friends are still alive, often they're elderly and not able to visit, so we become their family." If Fiona didn't watch out, that would be her when she died. All alone with no one to hold her hand or dry her tears. Fiona needed to call her mother and sister. Her visit home wasn't for a few more months.

"And people should be there for each other." Adelina looked at Fiona.

"I guess that's what Brice wants by asking us to be his witness-es for MAID. I guess that's what most of us hope—for someone to be there for us. You know, Adelina, asking couldn't have been easy for Brice. Neither of us has known him all that long. I don't understand why he asked us, but he did. I said I'd be there and I will."

"I want to be there to support Brice, Fiona. But MAID goes against so much of what I believe."

"I know, my friend, I know." Fiona stretched over the teapot and gave Adelina's hand a squeeze. "Whatever you decide, it has to be something you are comfortable with."

Brice

The Skype assessment with Dr Willmott, his MAID provider, went well—if a conversation about your impending death could be described as going well. Unlike his scholastic achievements, Brice ticked all the boxes. He was over eighteen years of age, he had a foreseeable death, he was doing this voluntarily, he could give consent, and he was part of the publicly funded healthcare system.

Because of their intimate circumstances, they had decided what they should call each other—Dr Janice and Brice. ("Mr Sanderson, are you ready now?" was like being called for your turn at the dentist.)

Brice was comfortable with Dr Janice carrying out his procedure, if procedure was even the right word. It did seem a little strange to Skype with the doctor helping you die. After all, death was pretty big on the most-significant-parts-of-your-life scale. But an appointment for a face-to-face would take two weeks. There was also the ten days reflecting period to consider after that meeting, and Brice didn't want to wait that long. He was ready.

It surprised him, after their talk, how light he felt. How happy.

How relieved. How energized. Emotions Brice had never associated with death before. Of course, he felt an intense sadness—he had ALS and he was going to die. But Brice felt blessed too. Blessed he could end his suffering and die peacefully. Blessed to be in control of his life. He looked over at his window. The sky was gently crying onto the glass. Grey, dull, rainy days of November, he wasn't going to miss. Now he'd get to spend Christmas with Peter.

Today was Monday. His MAID was scheduled in ten days. Brice had hoped to take the plunge on the Friday. It seemed fitting to be heading off one last time for the weekend. But Dr Janice had plans and wasn't available. So Thursday at 12:00 p.m. it was.

Brice thought back to his Skype with Sandy and Dave, two fellow renters from his old building. He needed two independent witnesses to sign his form and, for some reason, the two he chose were Sandy and Dave.

"Why us?" Sandy had asked.

Yes, why you? Oddly enough, his twenty-plus years of living in the apartment building with all its weirdos and marginalized inhabitants had been some of his best times. Strange, eccentric, irritating; they were family.

"I need two people to sign my form before I submit it. I'd like you and Dave to be my witnesses." This was all he managed to say as the tears and lack of muscle strength impeded his speech.

"Of course, we'll be your witnesses. When I think about how supportive you were fifteen years ago when I transitioned to a woman and needed a new job, I could cry. Brice, you helped me when a lot of people didn't want to talk to me, let alone touch me. You did my make-up and hair. Remember? You even stripped a mannequin from the women's designer section so I could have an outfit for my interview. Now it's this chick's turn to help you." Sandy moved closer to the computer screen. "You're one of the first people to accept me as the real woman I am."

Brice thought back to that time. So long ago. How could he not help? Transitioning to a woman, Sandy had faced some of the same challenges that he had being gay: Hate. Anger. Discrimination. Estrangement. All for being who she really was.

"I'll never forget how you came over the day after the tenants' unofficial meeting when we got our notices," Dave said, moving the screen to face him. "I was so hungover. I thought you were there to yell at me like everyone else. Instead, you just looked at me and gave me a hug. You were the mirror showing me what I was doing to myself. Then you came back with a schedule of the AA meetings your old boss attended. I've been on the wagon for almost six months now. It's my turn to be there for you." Dave looked into the camera. "We all have our struggles. It's having support that makes the difference."

Later that week, with the papers signed and the gossip shared, Sandy leaned into Brice as if sharing a secret. "I'm going to contact some of the old gang and plan a meet up. Except for Dave here, I haven't seen anyone from the old building since the renoviction. I didn't think I'd miss anyone from the old building, but I do. Even bratty Brian and his skateboard shenanigans. You know, even if people didn't understand my transition, most of them were very supportive. Surprisingly, the ones I thought would be the least accepting were the kindest." Crying, Sandy's mascara ran down her cheeks in black rivers. He watched as Dave handed her a tissue from the box in Brice's lap.

"Guess I'm going to miss the get together," Brice joked. "Lie to them. Tell them I look mah-ve-lous."

"All of us scattered like mice when the boot came down," Dave said. "When I was living there, I didn't realize how great our community was. But I do now. The place I'm in, you don't even get a good morning. Everyone just keeps their heads down, scrolling through their phones."

Brice sat in his wheelchair, watching from the lobby as Sandy and Dave walked away. The finality of his upcoming death loomed larger as his friends became smaller and disappeared from sight. Marcia was coming in from Ontario late Tuesday. The two of them would visit together Wednesday and Thursday morning. Marcia loved him, but attending his MAID or anyone else's was not something she was equipped to do. Morally or emotionally. Even with his terminal diagnosis, Marcia considered it suicide. Still, Brice had to give it to her: when Marcia saw his mind was made up, she hadn't tried to talk him out of it.

He'd decided against inviting anyone else. Thursday afternoon would be his last moment on earth, and he didn't want drama. This made him laugh. In the past he lived for drama. Drama was what made life interesting and exciting and fun. But now, he was so very tired. Fiona was coming and he still hadn't heard from Adelina. He just wanted to go in peace surrounded by his two new friends. Friends who, only having known him for a short while, had no preconceived ideas about who he was or what he'd done in the past, or much of anything else. They only knew this current version of Brice; an amalgamation of all the other Brices he'd been: son, brother, friend, husband, lover, homosexual, advocate, window designer, snappy dresser, wine and disco aficionado. A resident at

Calla Lily Tower who they'd helped on occasion. A caterpillar who wanted to leave his cocoon and fly away into something new and wonderful and beautiful.

It was almost laughable to him. Here he was at the end of his life and he finally had things in order. With almost no money left after what he'd spent on Azalea Tower, there was nothing in his will to change. He'd made the arrangements for the funeral director to send his body off to cold storage before it got cremated—one less thing for the MAID team to do. He also searched online for gay urns (who thought gay urns would be a thing?) and decided on one made of raku with the colours of the rainbow. Even dead, he'd be in fashion.

Fiona and Adelina had promised they'd throw his ashes into English Bay—one of his favourite places. He put some money aside for them to eat dinner at the Sylvia Hotel before they gave him a toss into the ocean. He hoped the night would be perfect for them.

Brice wasn't sure of the etiquette of sending out a death notice when you weren't dead yet. What was an obituary called for a pre-planned death? A ready-to-go? A pre-death? A pending? What would he say about himself? Great guy. A laugh a minute. Kind. Fun. Too bad he's dead. Couldn't have happened to a nicer guy.

But he did have the photo picked out. A great headshot, circa 1992 when he still had hair. He'd leave the obit for Marcia to do, with his help, of course. He didn't want her skirting around his being gay or his marriage to Peter.

Then there was the fun stuff. For his very last travel day around the sun, Dom Perignon. No way was Brice saying his good-byes with the too-sweet aftertaste of sparkling wine in his mouth. He only hoped he'd be able to drink a little without choking. Roses. Brice needed roses. Lots of them. Pink ones; their gentle fragrance wafting up to his nose as he left planet earth. Balloons too. He'd need lots of those in all the colours of the rainbow. A ginormous bunch outside his door in the shape of an arch letting everyone know: this is the room of a proud, gay man.

For music he'd start with Vivaldi's Four Seasons. Spring only. The whole year was a bit much. No question, his last song would be disco. He loved Gloria Gaynor's "I Will Survive," but it wasn't the best deathbed choice. So Brice was going out with Diana Ross and "I'm Coming Out." Leave 'em with that earworm to remember him by. Kindly, Waterview offered to provide some canapés for the guests. He looked over at his shamrock. A small, white, trumpet-shaped flower hiding within the green-purple leaves, a sign of life, had recently bloomed.

Adelina

Her cart rolled bumpily along. The requisition for repair was still in the to-be-done pile. Holly had been put on probation—hopefully, she'd get things on track with her sons before she lost her job. The new person filling in, Gigi, was nice enough. Thankfully, they both helped each other and shared the work.

Adelina continued down the hall toward Brice's room—she had thought long and hard about his request to be at his MAID, and her mind was made up. Medical assistance in dying went against her beliefs, but something inside her had grown from a spark into a raging fire. Time was passing and Brice needed an answer. She had Jesus's teachings to guide her—love thy neighbour as thyself.

Being there for Brice at such a difficult time, no matter what she felt personally about medical assistance in dying, was loving him. Adelina left her cart at the end of the hallway. She would go and see Brice and let him know her decision to be at his side.

Fiona

Fiona put the mascara wand back in the tube. She could sit there all day long applying mascara and it wouldn't do much more. Except continue her avoidance. The only other experience she might consider similar was when her cat Smokey needed putting down. There'd been no notice anything was wrong—just a howling cat and a surprisingly full kitty dish. An estimate of $1,200 and, at best, a month more of life wasn't enough of an upside for her, or the cat.

Fiona reached for her new green dress. She loved the blue trim along the collar and sleeves. She and Adelina had gone shopping on their day off. "Blue and green should never be seen," she sang, mimicking a primary school sing-song voice when the associate brought it over. The cost was more than Fiona had intended.

"It looks lovely. Quite the statement." The sales associate's gaze stopped at Fiona's scuffed and worn shoes—the support gone from years of jamming her feet into them like Cinderella's evil step-sisters. After taking the dress from Fiona, the clerk had nodded toward the escalator saying, "The shoe department is below us. Just turn left when you get off. Now follow me and we will get this rung up."

"Jeez, Adelina, I didn't know attending an assisted death was going to cost so much." Fiona tucked her new purse and shoes into the bag with her dress. Adelina's eyes opened wide. "OK, bad joke. What about you, have you seen anything you like?" Fiona had pictured them both as city gals strolling through downtown Vancouver, their paper shopping bags hanging off their elbows, the name of the semi-exclusive store turned outward for all to see. But Adelina only watched as Fiona dug through rack after rack, searching for her perfect dress. Now Fiona was outfitted and Adelina hadn't started looking.

"I think I have something at home that will be fine. You know, the dress I wore at Professor Moody's celebration."

"Maybe it's time for an update. Are you sure you don't want to look for something? The salesclerk told me there was a sales rack with some good deals. I'm sure we could find something for you. Let me give you something toward it."

"No. I don't need you to do that." Adelina looked so offended, Fiona wished she could take back her words. But her words were out there and Fiona knew if anyone deserved a new dress, it was Adelina.

"It's Don." Adelina's voice was a low whisper. "I don't think he'd be happy if I spent money on a new dress."

"Let's look anyway. I took so long deciding on my dress, they gave me the exclusive shopper discount on my next purchase just to get rid of me. We may as well use it. Brice's life is about fashion, Adelina. No way can we go looking like two frumps invited last minute to the jamboree. If we're going to be two of the last people Brice ever sees, we've got to look good." Fiona took Adelina's arm in hers and they marched off toward the sale racks where Adelina found a lovely deep pink linen dress.

"You can wear it with a jacket or a shawl to change the look," the same seasoned sales associate, well-versed in the frugal shopper's psyche, suggested. "You do look lovely in it."

"I could use a new dress for church," Adelina said, her hands smoothing out the fabric. Her face wore the hint of a smile.

"Come on Adelina, give us a spin." Fiona clapped her hands.

Adelina stood on her tip-toes and twirled before the three-way mirror. Looking at her, Fiona wondered if there was such a thing as happy eyes, because it seemed to her Adelina had them. "Let's make a true afternoon of this and go for a glass of wine at the lounge upstairs."

Three days later, dressed and ready to go, Fiona waited outside her apartment for her ride. The limousine Brice had booked for them was picking Adelina up first. Brice's sister Marcia was already with him, saying her final good-byes. Brice had explained to Fiona when she went in to check on him on her last night shift, "Marcia still thinks of it as committing suicide. But she loves me and supports me in my decision. She's visiting with me in the morning. She just can't be there when the time comes."

A long pink limo slowly maneuvered its way alongside the curb. The driver opened the door and Fiona climbed in and scooched across the seat to the far back across from Adelina. "Hello there, classy lady. You look lovely. How in heck did you get in here? It's so long!"

Adelina sat silently up against the side on the limousine, dwarfed by the plush leather seat. A champagne bottle stood at attention in a silver bucket of ice.

"Look! It's Dom Perignon!" Fiona gasped, lifting the bottle out of the ice and popping the cork. She poured champagne into two of the flutes. "I had Dom at a wedding once. An old friend married into money. It's like nothing else."

Fiona crawled over to Adelina, handing her one of the flutes, but Adelina shook her head. "You're awfully quiet Adelina." When there was no response, Fiona joked, "I'm not sure if this is the right thing to say, but, well, cheers!" Fiona tilted her glass and drank it down. Then, taking the glass of untouched champagne Adelina had declined, crawled her way to the back to her seat and started sipping on it. "Adelina, if I go for a third glass, stop me. I don't want to be the drunk at the party."

Too soon, their driver glided the pink limo to a stop before Calla Lily Tower.

Brice

The rainbow arch of balloons framed his door in a colourful show of pride. That morning, after his forever last bath and shave, Brice had asked Tonia to wheel him through his door. "Twice please. I need to get my money's worth," he joked. A few of the residents were clustered around Brice's doorway enjoying the joyful display of colours. Two asked if it was his birthday. Brice told them yes, and in a way it was. With his death, Brice was being born into something new.

The afternoon before, Marcia had arrived. She was staying at a nearby hotel. Things started out cautiously, like two people, with little in common, forced to sit beside each other at a dinner party. But the luxury of time to harbour ill feelings was gone. First thing, Marcia brought up Peter. Brice had braced himself for another uncomfortable conversation on the subject. Instead, Marcia confessed it had been hard for her to get used to the idea of two men marrying. Then she admitted something else to Brice: after seeing how much they loved and cared for each other, she was so happy that they had found each other.

In turn Brice learned things about Marcia he hadn't known before or bothered to ask. As their stories came out, the wall between them slowly crumbled. They talked about everything they could cram into a last afternoon together—their early lives, Brice's coming out, Marcia's getting married at eighteen to get out of their parent's house, her husband Sam and their great sadness at not being able to have children. They talked about her and Sam's plans to retire—sell the house, move to the cottage, exercise more, travel. So many of the things Brice had hoped to do and now never would.

By the time the sun set outside his window, Brice knew that, no matter what, Marcia was his sister, and he loved her. What surprised Brice that afternoon was that he also liked her.

Now, on his last morning, Marcia had arrived to say her final goodbye. They sat together quietly. Most everything had been said the day before. Marcia would stay a couple of days before heading home, to make sure things went well with his cremation and to deal with his estate and any other loose ends. She'd put the obituary he wrote in the newspaper.

"I can't believe this is our last time together, Brice. I never thought... honestly, I don't know what I thought. I guess I'm feeling scared. It's like that time at the fair when we got lost. We were so little. When you took my hand, I felt so safe. We walked and walked until you found that security guard. We kept calling him Mr Policeman. I'm sure it was only a few minutes, but it seemed like forever before he found Mom and Dad. Remember?"

Brice nodded.

"I'm deeply sorry I can't be there for your MAID, Brice. I just can't. I'm glad you understand. Just know I love you. Always have. Always will. I know we didn't see eye to eye on many things. I'll miss you so very much. May God watch over you as you make your way to heaven."

Marcia let go of his hand and got up. Bending over, she kissed him on the forehead before turning away and walking out the door. Brice heard her sob as she left the room, the balloons framing her in a rainbow of colour. He let her go. There was nothing he could do to comfort her.

Adelina

"Fiona, I am not sure if I can do this." Adelina looked down at Fiona who was doing her best to try and extricate herself from the limo.

"These things are really low to the ground. How does anyone get out of them with a stitch of grace? You seemed to slide your way out of here alright." Fiona held onto the door frame to help pull herself up. Her dress made its way up her thighs, showing off her new Spanx. "Adelina, we're here and you can do it." Fiona grunted. "Plus, we promised. Can you hold this bottle for a minute while I pull my dress down? I'm taking the champers with us. I'm sure we can have a glass with Brice before he heads off."

Adelina was not comfortable with this kind of talk—everyone sounding as if Brice was going on a vacation and not scheduled to die. Brice had said to her only the other night, "Adelina, all of us are here on this cosmic trip. Some have good times. Some have bad times. Some of us have too much baggage. Some not enough. Some get to stay for a long time. Some head off early. Me, I'm no longer having fun, and when that happens, next!"

This was not the way people should be talking about God's gift of life.

"Well, Adelina," Fiona said, as they stepped into the reception area, "this is it."

Dear God, Adelina silently prayed, *please give me strength to do this. I can't let Brice leave this world alone. Alone is such a sad place.*

Dr Janice

After picking up the necessary drugs from the pharmacy, Dr Janice met Nurse Christie outside the door of the director of care's office. Today's MAID would be Waterview's first. Janice held tightly onto her medical bag containing the drugs. Lethal, she needed them to be in her sight at all times. She was glad the team sent Christie. After completing eight MAIDs together, they'd gotten into an easy routine.

Janice looked over at Christie. "Ready?" Christie nodded her head. Janice knocked.

A professional woman in business attire opened the door. "Hello, please come in. I'm Susan White, director of Waterview Complex. I'm not sure which one of you I spoke to on the phone?"

"That was me. I'm Dr Willmott and this is Nurse Chalmers. Please call me Janice."

"And please call me Christie."

They sat down in the chairs offered.

"Our manager Theresa spoke with Brice about his MAID." Susan looked first at Janice and then at Christie. "Brice needed little help, having researched it on his own. He wanted to make sure Calla Lily Tower allowed MAID. Which of course is why you are here today. We're glad to be able to hold MAID in our facility. Since it was legalized, we've had a few people asking us about it, but so far, Brice is the first to go through with one. I know on the phone you said you didn't need anything, but please take my number, just in case." With that Susan handed Janice a card. Their meeting with the director finished, Janice and Christie stood to go. "Follow the arrows on the floor. When you see the balloons, you'll know you're there." The director shook their hands. "There's a bistro at the end of the hall should you need a coffee or tea. Please help yourselves."

"This is some doorway," Christie said, smiling at the rainbow balloon arch over the door to Brice's room. Janice took a deep breath before knocking. Although she'd completed this process twenty-five times before, meeting with patients prior to their MAID always caused some anxiety. Did the patient still want to go ahead with it? Last year, one had agreed, then changed their mind as the medications were being drawn up. Had their condition deteriorated so much that they could no longer agree to the procedure? Was everyone in attendance accepting of their loved one's choice? One family argued for over an hour until the patient told her adult children, "If you're not going to behave, you have to wait in the car." Everyone laughed and they behaved. Were there unreasonable expectations? After one patient passed, a distraught relative had asked if the drugs could be reversed.

Janice knocked.

"Come in." A voice, weak and slurred, answered.

"Hello, Brice. I'm Dr Janice and this is Nurse Christie. Nice to meet you in person." They both moved over to his hospital bed.

Even though they all knew what they were there for, this conversation was always difficult. A life was ending. "Before we proceed, I need to go through some formalities. I know you have friends joining you. Did you want me to wait for them to ask these questions or can we go ahead and get the process started?"

Brice nodded, his blue eyes clear and steady above his sharp cheekbones. All tucked into his hospital bed, Brice looked freshly showered. His bedside, tidy and uncluttered.

"You are Mr Brice Sanderson?"

"Yes."

"Are you agreeing to have the procedure known as medical assistance in dying or MAID, resulting in your death, performed on you today?" Janice listened closely as Brice, quietly answered:

"Yes, I most certainly am."

"OK, then we will proceed. Nurse Christie is going to start your intravenous. As we discussed in our Skype visit, we need the IV to give the medications to you which will result in your death. Are you agreeable?"

"I am."

"Brice, this shouldn't hurt," Christie said, looking at him. "After I wash the area with some alcohol, I'm going to give you a little poke with this needle." Christie held up the IV catheter to show him. "The needle inside retracts and this catheter stays in your arm. I then attach it to tubing which in turn is attached to this intravenous bag. It's only a little dextrose—basically sugar water, Brice. As Dr Janice explained, the intravenous is how the medications are administered. May I go ahead with inserting your IV?"

Janice watched as Christie expertly threaded the intravenous catheter up through Brice's vein. The movement reminded her of a snake sliding along the forest floor. Christie then attached the intravenous tubing to the catheter and slid the clamp on the tubing upward. Like drops from a tap not fully turned off, the solution started its slow drip into the chamber. Christie then taped the catheter at the site to secure it and taped the tubing further along his arm. "Good."

"Brice, as we discussed, I'm going to first administer a drug to sedate you. Then I will administer an anesthetic agent which puts you to sleep. Lastly, I will administer a paralytic agent that prevents you from breathing. I want to assure you that you won't feel any pain. After the medications are administered, it takes about ten minutes before death occurs. Do you understand?" Janice watched Brice nod his head, the movements flailing. ALS was a bitch. "Do you have anything you want to ask or say?"

"Thank you both for helping me." With great effort Brice turned his head to look first at Christie and then at her. "You're my angels of mercy."

"We'll leave you now. I know your friends are arriving soon and you'll want a visit. We'll be back at 1:30."

Janice closed the door to Brice's room. It was now 12:45 p.m. Christie headed off to the front lobby to call her husband about their dinner plans. Janice decided to take up the nursing director's offer and make a cup of tea. A life was ending and yet time continued to move for those still living.

As Janice waited for the kettle to boil, she went over the rest of her day in her head: Return any of the unused medications to the pharmacy. Pick up the kids from school. Go home. Change. Pack for the weekend. Buy groceries. Meet up with Paul at his law office.

Drive to the cabin. Relax.

Pouring the hot water into the teapot, Janice thought about how, at every MAID, she got to know her patients. Appreciate them. Mourn them. For some, even though she hardly knew them, she felt love. These losses took their toll. Somewhere there had to be a limitless well of strength into which she could dip and drink. She had been the attending physician at twenty-six MAIDs now. The first one was to observe and learn. The rest she'd performed. Each time was the same, yet different; a choreographed ballet leading to someone's death. There were either flowers or candles or balloons. At some point music played in the background. Most often it was something classical or easy listening. A couple of times there was jazz. Today Brice had chosen classical and disco—a rare combination for a rare man.

She thought of her kids. They would be happy about the balloons. Brice had promised all those attending they could take their pick of both the roses and the balloons. What was left would go to the Waterview lobby for the residents to enjoy. Roses and balloons. A joyful celebration or a morbid souvenir. It depended on how one saw this act of choiceful death.

Janice sipped her tea slowly. The warmth flowed down into her stomach. People seemed to think the brain or heart controlled the body, but it was in the stomach that so many emotions and ailments originated. Today the knot in hers was made of sadness, grief, love, and her appreciation for the time she had left in her own life. She drank another sip of her cooling tea.

If this were a movie, she might call it *An Afternoon of Death and Balloons*. But it was real life, and it was sad. ALS, a devastating deterioration, cutting a life short no matter how it ended.

She looked at her watch: 1:10 p.m. By 4:00 p.m. she'd have returned unused medications to the pharmacy. By 6:00 p.m. she'd be heading to the cabin with her family. Brice, she could only hope, would have found Peter and they would be dancing and laughing as if no time had passed between them.

A Medical Assistance in Dying Death

"Th-Th-The, Th-... That's all folks." Brice spluttered out his limited imitation of Porky Pig as Fiona and Adelina entered his room. "Sorry, can't do the whole thing."

"Dark, Brice. But funny." Fiona looked away. What did a person say at a time like this? *Can you do Bugs Bunny? Are you really sure you want to die today?*

"My, my, ladies, you both clean up well." Brice struggled to get the words out. "I hardly recognize you out of your uniforms. Please. Sit."

Adelina and Fiona sat on either side of his bed, each taking one of his hands.

"How was your ride?" His voice reminded him of a game of telephone. What started out in his head, morphed into something totally garbled and difficult to understand by the time it got out of his mouth.

"It was wonderful, Brice," Fiona answered. "I've never been in a stretch limo before. Champagne too! You went all the way!

Would you like a sip? There's lots left. Adelina didn't want any and I actually didn't drink it all."

Fiona poured some into a plastic cup he had at his bedside and tilted it to his lips. Brice took a small sip and then, starting to cough, moved his head away.

"That is a taste of heaven." Brice shook his head to a second sip.

Fiona looked around the room. "I love the balloons, and the roses are so pink. They smell great too." *Was she yammering?* "That's Vivaldi's Four Seasons isn't it? Is that Spring or Winter? I get those two mixed up. Actually, what am I saying? All the seasons sound the same, if you ask me." *Yes, she was definitely yammering.* Nerves did that to her.

"Brice," Adelina looked up from her bible, "I've chosen Psalm 23, 'The Lord Is My Shepherd.' It's such a beautiful prayer. I think it will bring you comfort as you make your way to heaven." She smiled gently as she wiped a tear from her cheek. "This is all so hard, Brice. We sit here making small jokes and talking like nothing is happening, but you are going to leave us."

"Yes, Adelina, it's hard. And it's good too. I need to go." The effort to speak made Brice feel like he was talking through a straw.

"I feel lucky." Fiona needed to speak her truth. "I never expected to meet such wonderful people as you both when I started working here." Laughing and sharing with others had been distant strangers to Fiona for so long. "Your MAID has got me thinking. I need to change some things. I don't know what I'm going to do, but I'm going to start enjoying more of my life while I have some left. Brice, I know you'll be busy up there checking out the heavens, but if you ever get the time, please send some good thoughts my way."

"Yes. I, too, have felt love for you both." Adelina looked at Fiona and then Brice, her body trembling like a small bird in a large hand. "I want to tell you both how much coming to Calla Lily Tower has meant to me too. God sent me here to meet both of you. Professor Moody too. Everyone here. Neither of you have ever made fun of me for my beliefs. You've both accepted me for who I am. I hope I have done the same for you." Adelina paused. "I need to tell you both something. Last week, the executor of Professor Moody's will contacted me. The professor left me some funds; such a sweet gesture to think of me on his last days." Adelina looked from Fiona to Brice. "We don't talk about what goes on at my house, but it's not good." Adelina's voice became quieter. "I asked God to guide me. I'm leaving Don. I've been thinking about it for a while and now, with the professor's generous gift, I'll have enough for a few months' rent on a new place and time to get on my feet. I wanted to tell you both this."

Fiona jumped in, the limo champagne making her brave. "I don't know if this is the right thing to say, but congratulations, Adelina!" Fiona had sensed things weren't right at Adelina's home and had tried a few times to get Adelina to talk, but her friend had remained silent. Now Fiona knew and she'd be there for her.

"Yes, Adelina," Brice said, the spittle coming from his mouth making it more difficult for him to speak and to be understood. "You're going to shine." Fiona wiped his mouth.

Silent, they sat there waiting. Adelina and Fiona each still holding one of Brice's hands, not to keep him there, but to anchor themselves. All of them afraid to look at the clock as if that would prevent time from passing. But pass it would, and Brice would be gone, and they would go on. Seconds later the knock came and the door opened. Dr Janice entered the room, Christie behind her.

"Brice, are you ready? It's time."

Addendum

This story takes place in 2019. Since that time, there have been changes to the Canadian MAID program. For further information visit:
https://www.canada.ca/en/health-canada/services/medical-assistance-dying.html.

As well, you can contact your local health authorities for further information.

For anyone experiencing domestic abuse, there is help:
https://www.canada.ca/en/public-health/services/health-promotion/stop-family-violence/services.html

For further information on ALS in Canada:
https://als.ca

Acknowledgements

To everyone at The Self Publishing Agency—Megan, Ira, Anna. There is no better team of people to guide me through the perils and tribulations of writing and self-publishing. Extra special thanks to Tara McGuire, my editor, for her many—and I do mean many—thoughtful edits, helping to make my book the best it can be. Thank - you also to Elise Volkman, proof-reader, for all her expert changes.

To both Yasmine Franchi and Petya Tsankova my book designers. WOW!

To Mary and Varteres, who have both been supportive and patient through not only the writing of this book, but have also helped to guide me through the snarl of social media. There's a special place in heaven for friends like you.

To Anne, author of *An Angel in the Marble: What Breast Cancer Taught Me*, who got me into self-publishing when she asked, "If not now, when?" Thanks for the push and for being my friend.

To my sisters and all my friends, I only hope the love and support you have given me, I have returned back to you. Thanks.

To Tere, you're the wind beneath my wings. Couldn't have done it without. You're an inspiration and guiding light. There's no one better.